Rare S

an A-Z anthology of short fiction

Liam Bell

Bridge House

British Library Cataloguing in Publication Data
A Record of this Publication is available from the British
Library

ISBN 978-1-914199-38-7

This edition published 2023 by Bridge House Publishing
Manchester, England

Rare Stories:
an A-Z anthology of short fiction

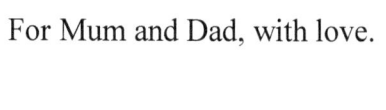

For Mum and Dad, with love.

Contents

Through a six-month period, I wrote a sequence of thousand-word stories inspired by entries marked as "rare" in the Oxford English Dictionary. They were written, posted online weekly and presented here as A-Z but they can be read in any order. There is one substitution, from the original sequence, and those listed below have been published, in one form or another, in the following places:

"babblative" in *Honest Ulsterman* (as "Service Charge")
"deericide" in *Northwords Now*
"flatter-blind" in *Honest Ulsterman*
"philobiblian" in *The Bookseller* (as "On Second Hand Bookshops")
"umbratic" in *Freckle Magazine* (as "In the Event of Landing on Water")

apple-squire (noun):

a male companion of a woman of ill-repute

Glyn knew that they talked about his wife. Not just the houses immediately next door, but the ones either side of those too. And further. It was what came of living in a cul-de-sac. Gossip swilled back-and-forth, with no through-road.

She made it worse for herself, Joan, by staring out at the children playing on the street; the six-year-old from number twelve and the seven-year-old, with the three-year-old brother, from number seventeen. They saw her peering from the edges of the curtains and they squealed and ran to tell their parents.

He heard the kids talking in stage-whispers. The woman in number fourteen, they said, has three baths a day. Her recycling is all empty wine bottles. She eats spiders from the corner of the ceiling and snails from the plant pots. The hoover stands in the hall all day, unused. The lights are on at 3 am because darkness turns her into a creature with bat's wings and dragon's breath.

The parents were initially kind. That was quite a few years ago. They offered to do a shop, to save Glyn from going, and invited both of them over for a drink on New Year's Day. Soon, though, there'd been a note through the door asking them to trim the front grass and then another suggesting the name of a man who could clear the gutters.

'We could move,' Glyn suggested. 'A bungalow, maybe?'

'I'm not ready.'

'Of course not, love.'

Part of him was relieved. A bungalow was best saved for retirement. So he settled for calling the gutter-man and negotiating a fixed price that included repainting the back fence and fixing the cracks in the driveway.

9

'She's still young,' Edwina from number six said to him, one evening as she took out her black bin bag. She'd also had notes through the door, because she overstuffed the wheelie bin and often left loose bags at the side. 'You're still young.'

'Perhaps. We'll have to see,' Glyn said. 'It's Joan's choice.'

'Shall I call in for her, in the daytime? For coffee, maybe.'

'I'll ask her. Thank you.'

'She has my phone number.'

The foxes would get at Edwina's bins. There would be further complaints, the council might even be called. She didn't seem to mind, though. Her house was at the curve of the street; she could see a slice of the main road.

The Fultons, in number fifteen, moved out and the teenagers were replaced with eight-year-old twins. The other kids migrated into their garden. There was a climbing frame and a trampoline. They kept one eye on Joan, at the window, and she was integrated into their games whenever there was a call for a villain: wicked witch, spy, assassin, Prime Minister. It would have been useless to explain that Joan was staring only at the bare, uneven flowerbeds in her own garden.

It all got worse in Autumn. Not only the nights drawing in, but also overactive imaginations at Halloween. No guiser called at number fourteen. They knew they wouldn't get any sweets, any chocolate.

Two days into November, Joan sat down at the kitchen table and wrote a card. She sealed it, in a red envelope, before Glyn had the chance to read it or even glimpse the message on the front. Later, when she was in the bath, he opened the drawer beneath the kettle and found four other envelopes, one for each year that had passed.

'Love,' he tried the next day, 'would you like to try for a job, maybe, or you could go back to studying? An exercise class, even…?'

'I don't need exercise, Glyn.'

'It might help.'

'You tell me I don't eat enough…

'It's not about weight.'

'Quiet,' she closed her eyes. 'Please.'

The house deteriorated further. The quince bushes grew too big and pushed through the fence into next door. The twins started to lob the fruit up towards Joan's window. The double-glazing rattled and she stepped away.

In the utility room was a disorderly regiment of glass bottles, upright among the chaos of cardboard and the towels which hadn't made it into the dryer. Glyn felt he could only leave out a few at a time, with the recycling. One dark evening, he'd pile the rest of them into the quince bushes or bury them at the edge of the grass.

The young boy, from number seventeen, was now an inquisitive five. He ran lengths of the cul-de-sac in bare feet. As Glyn walked home, he sprinted up behind.

'You're the man from that house,' he said, pointing.

'Yes.'

'My sister says there are cameras. That you record us.'

Glyn spluttered. 'We record…?'

'She says you write down every move we make.'

'Certainly not.'

He shrugged, 'I'm too fast anyway.'

The boy turned and ran off. Glyn found that it took three attempts to fit his key into the lock and when he tried to call Joan's name there was a quiver to his voice.

'What is it?' she called back.

'We need to do something.'

'Like what?'

11

Glyn walked into the hallway. He lifted the hoover and set it back in its cupboard. Then he went to the kitchen and got a black bag from beneath the sink. He shoved all of the bottles from the utility room in it, then the cardboard and the mouldering towels. As he lifted the bag, there was a noise like a window shattering.

Five years ago, he would have eased the front door open only wide enough for him and the bag. He would have made sure it was closed behind. There wasn't much traffic in the cul-de-sac, but the cars sometimes swung around the corner at quite a speed.

Glyn lifted the bag into the wheelie bin, the one for general waste. He tipped the bin onto its wheels and walked it to the kerb. Edwina was there, black bag in hand.

'I never did hear from Joan,' she said.

'No, she still struggles.'

'All of that though…' Edwina avoided his eye. 'Seems an awful fuss to make over a wee dog.'

Glyn looked back at the houses behind them. The twins at number fifteen were up at the window, looking out. The one from number twelve was there too. She didn't duck away like the others.

'The question that torments Joan,' Glyn said slowly, 'is how he got the chocolate? We should have been more careful.'

Edwina tied another knot in her black bag. 'One of those things,' she said.

'We should have taken better care of him.'

'No one blames you,' Edwina replied. 'I shouldn't think.'

babblative (adj.):

given to babbling; loquacious, prattling

Let me tell you about Fiona McIntyre. That's her there, parking her silver BMW convertible on those double-yellow lines. Her hair went grey in prison, but it's back to coiffured copper-red under that headscarf. Dipping her sunglasses, she looks beneficently around Ann Street. As if her perfume is the sea-breeze that ripples through the town, as if her mere presence is the reason the locals step out of their front doors.

Which, in a way, is true. Folk around here love to catch sight of Fiona. If only so that they can turn, scandalised, to the person behind them in the bakery queue or scuttle across The Diamond to where the taxi man smokes his cigarettes. *Can you believe—?* They say. *The sheer brass neck on her—*

She steps towards the butcher's shop and all eyes follow her. She knows it too; throws in a little sashay of her hips in her floral summer dress. Those waiting inside shuffle back a step. Big Gerry the butcher clears his throat and tries for a smile. There's no blame attached to him – he has to make his living. Beneath the counter, out of sight of the sausages and chops, is the wagyu steak he's ordered in specially for Miss McIntyre. It bleeds against its greaseproof wrapping. He hands it over and takes her tainted money in return. For the rest of the day, he'll avoid meeting the eye of his other customers.

From here, Fiona will make her way from shop to shop, as she has every day since her release, leaving behind this trail of embarrassment and resentment. You could say jealousy – you might be tempted – but there are few in Ballycastle who'd swap places with her. Or, at least, few who'd do what she did; who'd betray their friends and neighbours.

A few years back, Fiona was just another one of us. She lived up Moyle Road and drove a wee scabby hatchback back and forth to her job at the bank. Only a counter job, nothing more. It was Mr Smyth who came up from Coleraine two days a week to approve the loans, deal with the mortgage arrears and extend overdrafts. Fiona was the one the majority of folk saw, though, for their day-to-day deposits and withdrawals: sliding a tenner into a grandson's savings account on pension day, sending over a wee rent payment to a daughter in Scotland, filling an envelope for a tradesman.

She was well-liked, is the truth of it. Turned out in her uniform, with the name tag on the pocket of the white-shirt and the blue necktie neatly knotted. Her hair was all split-ends, but she kept it tied back and tucked in behind her ears. And she always had a word of sympathy for those suffering with creaking hips or recent grief. She'd gone to the school opposite the chapel and taken the job in the bank straight after her exams. Everyone had known her mum and dad, who'd passed within three months of one another – hard to remember which one went first – and left her that semi-detached house up Moyle Road.

If there was anger at the introduction of a service charge then it was directed at the bank's head office rather than at Fiona. Mr Smyth was only in one day a week, by that point, and his skin was the colour of seagull-shit with the stress of the closure of the Portrush branch, so no-one thought to query the charge with him. It was only a pound-fifty, after all, and – as Fiona said – it was a small price to pay for the convenience of actually having a bank in the town.

The locals adapted and swapped tips on how to avoid being stung for too much: *lift enough to last you the week, Mary; they take card in the coffee shop now, love, and you can just hold it against the machine there; our Caitlin can show you how to use the online thingummy now, Patrick, if it's just a transfer...*

So, the majority of folk swerved the worst of it, even as the charge crept up to two-pounds and then two-fifty. And it was agreed that the wait in the bank was more manageable now and that Fiona was growing into a fine young woman who'd be running the head office in a few years. The efficiency of her was a sight to behold: the way she could quote you reams of terms and conditions without even lifting her eyes from the computer screen, could keep up the chatter even as she wetted her thumb to count out the notes, apply the relevant number of service charges with just a tap of a manicured nail on the keyboard.

It was the trips away that set the tongues wagging. Fiona suddenly having the money for jaunts down to Belfast and Dublin, even weekend stays over in Glasgow and London. She always came back with a full bloom of shopping bags on each arm and something subtly improved about her hair or nails or eyebrows. Then she swapped out her hatchback for the convertible and filled the passenger seat with a succession of hipster-lads who looked at the menu in the café as if it were written in a different language and who sighed when the barmaid in the local explained that it was only *Harp* and *Guinness* they had on draught.

The charge got to three-twenty before someone remarked on it. Even then it was more an accident than anything. Mrs Bryson was having to remortgage to pay for a care home for her father. He had dementia, they reckoned. Anyway, she got herself in to see Mr Smyth and – in passing – asked if the three-twenty would be charged in this instance: *Only it's not a new mortgage, is it? Or not a new transaction, at least. And there's these other fees involved and—*

Word spread quickly. It was well-known that the police

had been summoned, even before Mr Smyth ended the call to them. And the suited man from head office must have found it strange to have his car greeted by a wee cluster of locals who seemed eager to follow him up the street to the bank.

Fiona was taken off the counter, of course, and replaced by an older woman with a brisk manner and a Belfast accent. Her nametag was a scrawl – maybe Susan or Sasha. Several dog-walkers took it upon themselves to re-route up Moyle Road, to have a look at the drawn-curtains and closed gate of the McIntyre house. *New PVC windows*, they reported back. *And was there always a Velux in the roof there? Hard to see, but is that new tiling in the kitchen at the back?*

It didn't take long for the bank to trace the payments. Fiona was no Canary Wharf whizz, after all, no criminal mastermind with knowledge of offshore accounts or shell corporations. She *was* a criminal though, it was decided. A day in court and then a year inside. For fraud. For skimming that small amount off every single transaction that took place in our town over the course of eighteen months or so.

The bank recovered some of the money, of course, but the locals would have to bring a separate civil case for the money *they'd* lost. And, here's the thing, not one single person had been taken for more than a couple of hundred pounds. Not one person had been swindled enough to justify the lawyer's fees. We could have banded together, perhaps, but that takes a lot for a town where grudges are still held about a borrowed lawnmower unreturned ten years later, an invite to a golden wedding anniversary allegedly lost in the post, and a husband who strayed from his wife with the man who delivers the sheep feed.

Anyway, come here a bit closer to hear the real question. The real crux of the matter. This is the thing that should matter more than Fiona swanning around like King Midas or the fact that head office will be closing our branch within the month. It's this that's important to ask. Although don't feel you need to answer if it makes you uncomfortable. You're a newcomer to this community, after all, and it's important to fit in. It's important, maybe, that you hate Fiona with the passion that the rest of them do. But answer this – *why was no-one bothered when it was assumed that the bank was taking the money? Where was the outrage then, eh? Why did it belong with them any more than in the pocket of our own Miss McIntyre?*

combuster (noun):

a person or thing that causes combustion

'It's probably nothing.'

'What's probably nothing?'

'Just that when we go for food—'

'He doesn't chew with his mouth open, does he?'

'No, not that. His table manners are fine... well—'

'Shit. He's one of those guys who's an arsehole to waiters, right?'

'No. It's just that he'll only order beige food.'

'What?'

'Pasta, or potato, or bread.'

'Carbs?'

'Well, he'll eat cauliflower or, like, panna cotta.'

'Fuck.'

'And the waitresses all make that face you're making right now.'

'That face, darling, is called *disgusted and appalled: a portrait.* You could hang it in an art gallery. I mean, what kind of serial killer only eats white food?'

'Beige.'

'That's worse.'

'How?'

'Well, it's not fucking better, is it?'

'It's only a small thing, though.'

'Break it off. Now. Get your phone out of your pocket and send him a message. Right. Now.'

'He's lovely, though.'

'Can you imagine anything freakier? Would he eat, like, a carrot, maybe? If it'd been boiled down until all the colour leeched out of it... or, is that worse? That is worse. A fucking anaemic carrot.'

'We met at a silent reading party.'

'Oh well, I take it back then. No psycho would *ever* go to an event in a pub where every sad-sack is sitting reading without even a whisper of conversation. He's fine then. Nothing to worry about.'

'You're a sarcastic bitch.'

'And he's a serial killer.'

'It is a bit embarrassing. The food thing.'

'Darling, it's downright psychotic. He only eats white food. Is he a fascist? I bet he is – I bet he's a fucking fascist. Wait… does that mean he only eats white chocolate?'

'He doesn't eat dark chocolate, no.'

'White chocolate. Darling. *White* chocolate.'

'But he's very sweet—'

'You would be too—'

'And we're into all the same things: hillwalking and reading and nights on the sofa and—'

'And thunderstorms… *Everyone* puts those things on their dating profiles.'

'We met in person, though.'

'And – wait – what about the sex? If he's not into anything except beige on the plate, then there can't be much imagination in that department, am I right? A flavoured condom must be his worst nightmare.'

'It's not flavour he has a problem with.'

'So it's strictly standard johnnies, is it?'

'Well, we've not actually got that far yet. That was only our third date on Friday and we just… well, we spoke about it and—'

'You *spoke* about it? Darling, you and I do nothing but speak about it. That's not his *purpose*, my love, that's not his *function*. No, dump him. If you don't, then I'll do it for you. In fact, give me your phone. Give it here. What's his name? Is he in your contacts?'

'You're not dumping Mark.'

'No, *you* are. I'm just your facilitator.'

'We had a kiss. We said we'd wait to take it further. Until the next date, until we could have the house to ourselves.'

'Wait, what? *This* house, the one you share with *moi*?'

'Is that not ok?'

'Is it ok that you're bringing a serial killer home from a silent reading party, so that you can have silent, beige sex and he can strangle you in your sleep? Is that ok? Hmmm. Will I come back to find the walls painted beige and the cat fucking bleach-blonde?'

'He's not going to strangle me. All you know about him is that he eats beige food. He's so nice otherwise.'

'Did he have a childhood trauma with a curry, is that it? Or choke on some red jelly or something? I mean, what kind of – ?'

'Actually, I think it was to do with when he was younger.'

'Dump him. Now.'

'I think he had problems with his stomach, with his digestion. He didn't tell me the full story, but he was in-and-out of the hospital with it. Everything he ate seemed to react and he was surviving on nothing but *Lucozade* – for the glucose – but then even that started to give him a stomach ulcer. So they gave him some porridge and he put on some weight. Then he moved on to bread and that, and – what are you doing?'

'Looking for him on *Facebook*.'

'Why?'

'Is it Mark Storey, is that him?'

'Don't you dare—'

'Must be, you've only been friends a fortnight.'

'Are you just having a look?'

'Nope, I'm posting on his wall.'

'What – ? Give it!'

'Can't. Too late.'

'What the hell. What did you write?'

'You'll thank me, darling.'

'You've posted a link, have you? It's a recipe for lamb tagine… You bitch.'

'If he makes it for you – if he eats it – then you'll know he's the one. If not, then not. You're welcome.'

'It could literally kill him.'

'You're so over-dramatic.'

'Have you not been listening? He had problems with his stomach as a kid, they had to cut some of his intestines away, I think. He couldn't go to school. They were genuinely fearful that it might kill him.'

'First of all, I wasn't listening. I was trying to remember how to spell tagine. Right? Second of all, if it's something that he can't help then it seems a bit harsh to judge him for it, darling. Like, if it's not just a weird phobia – if it's actually *physical*.'

'Exactly, but you've just posted on his wall.'

'At least see what he's like in bed first…'

'A fucking recipe for lamb tagine.'

'Maybe avoid seeing him at mealtimes.'

'I'll have to explain that I told you.'

'It seems like it's basically nothing to worry about.'

'I am worried. What do I tell him?'

'Not that – the beige food thing.'

'You really think?'

'Yeah, it's probably nothing.'

deericide (noun):

the killing or killer of deer

After the last exam, Gemma sat with her father in the pebbled garden and looked up at the pine trees on the hillside. The last of the sun squinted through. Her father sipped on a beer, but she shook her head when he offered it.

'I know the last year's been tough,' he said. 'At school.'

'Not just the last year.'

'All of it,' he nodded. 'I know.'

Gemma tried a smile; no-one could ever make her go back.

'I'm proud of you,' her father said. 'Your mum would have been too. For making the effort. Those kids… life isn't like that. You'll find friends, there'll be folk who'll share your interests.'

'My interests?' Gemma frowned.

'Not all of them. But board games or history books…'

'Ah, the *normal* ones.'

Her father took a drink of beer. 'You remember that hideous deer-thing you found when we first moved in. Grotesque bloody thing.'

'Darren.'

'Yes, you called it Darren.'

Gemma had found Darren on the shelf in the cluttered shed. He must have been left by the previous owner. He was a tiny fallow deer, the size of a kitten, curled inside a sealed bell-jar and preserved in some greenish liquid. You could see the outline of the muscles, of the jawbone, beneath orange and white hair. The ears were exquisite. And his eyes were closed, as if in sleep.

'What made you think of him?' Gemma asked.

'I worried… for a spell… about the attachment you had to it.'

22

She had trundled Darren around the garden in the wheelbarrow and taken him down to the stream. There they used sticks to build a raft that wouldn't float and then a pyre that wouldn't burn. At night, she placed him on the windowsill so that he could see the stars, if he ever opened his eyes. Gemma lay in bed wondering what the greenish liquid would smell like, if she opened the jar, or if, once it drained away, the deer would shake itself and rise unsteadily on stick-thin legs. Like Bambi finding his feet on the ice.

'That was the summer after your mother,' her father said, 'and I worried that you might want to take it to school – you took it everywhere. Things were bad enough, I'm not sure anyone could have protected you if they'd found a taxidermied deer in your schoolbag.'

'I don't think Darren was taxidermied.'

'Sorry?'

'He wasn't stuffed, he was preserved. He was whole.'

'Embalmed then.'

Gemma nodded, accepting the word. She took a twist of her hair and set it between her teeth. Then she let it fall, because her father hated that habit. She looked across; he hadn't noticed.

'We got through it,' he said. 'All of it. And now you can go off and find something you want to do. With decent people, folk who'll just leave you be.'

'Like what?'

'Sorry?'

'What can I do?'

'Well, what would you like to do?'

Gemma had once thought of working with animals. Not as a vet, but in a cat shelter or a pet store. Darren had been supportive, but he wanted her to aim higher. Maybe History at university, if she could avoid group-work and presentations.

She'd taken Darren on the bus, in her schoolbag, to Glasgow and found the building where they taught it. She didn't speak to anyone, but she got a leaflet. Then they'd wandered in the Hunterian Museum, where Darren's brethren stared down from the shelves; dozens of bell-jars with all kinds of different animals, both taxidermied and embalmed.

'He wasn't grotesque,' she said to her father.

'Who wasn't?'

'Darren.'

'It was a tiny deer in a jar, Gemma.'

'If he had been a doll, though, or a cuddly toy...'

'Then I'd have accepted you taking it to bed with you, or setting it on the table while you ate. A cuddly toy in your bike basket is normal, a dead deer is not.'

'There's that word again.'

'What word?'

'Normal.'

Gemma placed some strands of hair in her mouth. Just a few. This time, her father saw. He gave her a look, so she let them fall. The look softened.

'Listen honey,' he said, 'I was genuinely worried about that deer. And there was enough... I thought it was worth your being upset for a few days if it spared you some torment at school.'

'What do you mean?'

Her father sipped his beer. The sun had gone. Gemma felt it not as a single shiver, but as a spreading chill. She remembered the morning she'd lost Darren; the search starting as frantic, switching to methodical, and then reverting to frantic.

'What did you do with Darren?' she hissed.

'I took it up into the woods. The idea was to empty the jar, so the thing could rot naturally. But the seal was tight.

24

And when I tried to smash it, the jar bounced up off the pine needles.'

'So…?'

'So I buried it. In the jar.'

'You know where he is?'

'We'd never find it now.'

Gemma waited until her father met her eye. 'You're sick,' she said.

Her father raised himself from the seat, lifted the empty beer bottle. Before he turned his back, Gemma took a fistful of hair and stuffed it into her mouth. He passed no comment on that.

'It was for the best,' he said, instead.

Gemma shook her head, kept her stare focused on the silhouetted trees on the hillside. She heard her father's sigh, the crunch of his shoes on the pebbles.

Tomorrow was the first day. She wouldn't spend it typing up a CV or searching online for college courses. Instead, she would go into their neatly-ordered shed and look out a spade. Then she would go up to the woods and start digging. Hole after hole. And when she found him, she'd tell him all the things she'd saved up over the years. Things that would finally open his eyes.

emacity (noun):

fondness for buying

> *Miniature Brass Carriage Clock, £49.00*
> *Polaroid 600 Instant Camera, £21.78*
> *Organic Chai Seeds, £10.39*

We moved in with my mother after the flat sold, so that we could save up a larger deposit. It was Claire's idea, but that didn't stop her complaining. 'Your mum just *hovers*,' she said, 'as I wash the dishes or sort the recycling. She never passes comment, I could take that. Instead she just watches, following me from one room to the next, like a cat waiting for its food to be put out.'

I didn't speak up for my mum. It was her house we were invading and she was used to being on her own, but Claire needed to be able to vent. The commute to work was longer from Mum's and she was drained from those late nights on the laptop, looking at property sites and god-knows-what-else. So, I kept quiet and tried to distract my mum with those Nineties game-shows she likes to watch.

Three weeks in, though, I got a text from the chap who'd bought the flat saying that there were three parcels waiting for us. It took me a few days before I drove out, after work, to collect them. By the time I did, another two had arrived.

> *Hennessy Paradis Cognac, £499.95*
> *Morphy Richards Breadmaker, £79.99*

In the car, I unwrapped them by size. The small ones – the chai seeds and the camera – seemed like they might be Claire, but the other three were odd. Especially the brandy.

When I walked in with the breadmaker in my arms, Claire was delighted. Then she scolded me for buying gifts when we were supposed to be saving. I explained that I hadn't ordered them and she pointed out that they were plainly addressed to me. I couldn't fault her logic, but it didn't change the fact that neither of us had ordered them. Claire picked at the wax seal on the cognac and turned to my mum, who was in the utility room worrying the corners of the folded sheets.

'Did you order these things?' Claire asked.

'What a nice surprise, love. I like the carriage clock,' Mum said.

'Did you buy them, though?'

'Of course not,' I said. 'They came to the old flat.'

Four of the sellers listed only a postal address, but the cognac had an email address as well. The reply to my email came two days later. It said the bottle had been bought through an auction website. At the bottom of the email was the price. I calculated that each measure we'd had was worth eighteen pounds.

My mum stood in the dining room while I flicked through the tabs Claire had left open on the laptop. The auction site was one of them. As I checked it, Mum reached out to the orchid on the windowsill and rubbed the petals between her finger and thumb. Then she followed me out to the hall, where I phoned the bank. I'd cut up the credit card, but never cancelled it. I explained this to the bank, while mum re-straightened the lines of shoes by the door. The girl on the phone told me the card had been used only the day before, for three more purchases.

Kitchen Table, Bare Wood, £37.00
Antique Wood Sideboard Cabinet, £222.00
Pair of Gothic Revival Chairs, £110.00

I texted, the next day, to warn the guy in our old flat and he replied to say that they'd already arrived. Then he added a laughing emoji. That confused me a little, but I was in the van rental place at the time so I didn't reply.

When I went to pick them up, though, I found only three tiny packages. They could all fit comfortably on the passenger seat. I drove home with only dust-sheets and strappings in the back.

'They're for a doll's house,' I shouted as I came in.

'What?' Claire was at the door to the living room.

'Doll's furniture. You can hold them in your hand.'

She burst out laughing, but my mum – standing just behind her – was shaking her head and squeezing a sofa-cushion between her hands like it was a concertina.

'Mum?' I said.

'They should list dimensions, sweetie.'

'What do you mean? Was this you?'

'You guess the price, you see,' she said, 'and if you win then they send it to you.'

'So… it was?'

'You were so happy with the breadmaker, but… they should have listed the dimensions for these ones.'

Claire had covered her mouth, but she was still smiling. I would have expected her to be furious. Instead, she lifted one of the packages and tore it open. When she pulled out one of the Gothic chairs, she had to kneel down on the floor with the laughter coming like convulsions.

'Mum,' I softened my voice, 'did you not hear me on the phone to the bank? Did you not hear us when we were talking about the first lot of parcels?'

'Oh dear,' she said. 'I don't like to interfere.'

'But you knew you'd bought all those things.'

'Not bought, darling, won.'

'No, bought.'

She frowned. Then looked down at the cushion as if seeing it for the first time.

'You know I don't understand computers, love,' she said.

'Come on,' Claire took a breath, 'let's get a glass of cognac and we can have a seat on these nice new chairs you bought.'

My mum looked upset at that, so I led her away from the fresh screams of laughter and back into the living room. I flicked on *Challenge TV* and there was Bruce Forsyth.

'You see,' mum said, pointing. 'Like the gameshow.'

'Yes, mum. Not quite the same, though.'

Back out in the hallway, I sat myself down on the floor beside Claire. She held out one of the chairs, presumably intending to repeat her joke. She couldn't even get the words out.

'This furniture she bought,' I said, 'is too small for this house, you know.'

'You don't say...'

'I'm saying, though, that she might need to downsize.'

Claire stopped laughing, looked up.

'We wouldn't buy her a doll's house,' I said, 'but something more manageable.'

'Bigger than a doll's house, smaller than this place.'

'Exactly.'

'Somewhere she can make her own chai seed bread?'

Claire smiled.

'We'd make sure she has everything she needs, yes.'

'Shall we have a quick look online?'

'I'll get the cognac.'

flatter-blind (verb):

to flatter so as to make blind; to blind with flattery

I picked the pub, along the seafront, with the frosted glass. The view from the holiday let was out over Fairhead and Rathlin Island, and I'd had my fill. All I wanted to see was a pint and the wood of the bar.

On the next stool along, though, was a chatty sort. He had a whisky in front of him. As soon as I ordered my *Guinness*, he looked over.

'Not from around these parts,' he said.

'Scotland,' I nodded.

'Business or pleasure?'

'Neither. Both.'

He turned towards me; always a bad sign. His clothes were those of a farmer – wax jacket, corduroy, stout boots – but a well-turned-out version.

'What is it you do?' he asked.

'I'm a writer.'

'Is that so? What sort of thing do you write about?'

'The usual – death and sex.'

'Is that so?'

'Aye. I'd welcome one, but the other is likely years off...'

He chuckled. 'I'm closer to one than the other, right enough.'

I nodded again, but was spared further conversation by the arrival of two men in their thirties. They wore high-vis jackets. One went to the barmaid, the other straight over to my new friend. I didn't mean to overhear, but the bar was quiet enough.

'Evening Mr Henderson,' the high-vis man said.

'Evening lad.'

'I'll get you a drink in. What'll it be? A short?'

The man signalled and two drinks became three. He didn't acknowledge me, but I was planning to be on my way shortly in any case.

'That car of yours still giving you trouble, lad?' Mr Henderson asked.

'It is, aye. The fan belt, they say.'

'Is that so?'

'An expensive fix, Mr Henderson, near four hundred.'

'Well, you stood me a drink.'

I lifted my eyes and saw the barmaid set a whisky on the bar. In the same moment, Mr Henderson took a chequebook from his inside pocket, scribbled in it and tore out the cheque. He handed it to the man in the high-vis jacket.

Over the next hour, the next two pints, I saw the self-same thing happen twice more. I should have gone for the walk I was planning, along the beach, or returned to the chapter I was writing, but this was far more interesting. Someone would come in, go over to my new friend and offer to buy him a drink. He would accept, make conversation and the newcomer would give some sob-story that had him reaching for the chequebook. He gave a woman in her fifties two-hundred for a new washing machine and an elderly gent seventy-five for his gas bill.

I thought of my bank balance, of the advance that had petered out to only three figures. This trip, then I'd need to look for some freelancing.

The pub was two rooms and, after receiving their cheques, each of the supplicants shuffled off to the back room. There was an occasional draught of laughter from under the door.

Mr Henderson sat silent and slumped for a while, with me watching him sidelong, then he stirred as the front door opened. This one was a youngster, looked no more than fifteen, in the kind of shiny tracksuit that would catch fire at the sight of a candle.

'Well, Hugh,' he said.

'Well, Pinky,' Mr Henderson replied.

'I'm needing a new laptop for college.'

'Is that so?'

'They cost two grand, so they do.'

'Buy me a drink, lad.'

Young Pinky went to the barmaid and Hugh lifted his chequebook. I cleared my throat. Laptops don't cost two grand, I wanted to say, this young one's a chancer. Instead I waited until the transaction was over and Pinky was through in the back room.

'Forgive me,' I leaned across. 'But... two thousand?'

Hugh chuckled. 'Bit steep, eh?'

'He could get one for a few hundred.'

'I don't doubt it.'

Hugh had both hands around his glass. I noticed that the previous two still had their measure of whisky in them, untouched.

Now, normally, I wouldn't interfere. I mean, I don't know the ins-and-outs. All these scroungers might be of the Henderson family, for all I knew. Nevertheless, three pints in, I needed to find out.

Standing, I made my way to the back. If I was challenged, I could always say I was looking for the toilet. From the other side of the door came words I couldn't make out: a punchline, then laughter. I took a breath, pushed the door.

There were three tables. The gas-bill gent sat at one, the washing machine woman was with a friend at another and, around the last, Pinky had joined the high-vis men. They all looked up.

'He's come to say something,' Pinky said, with a grin.

'Pardon?'

'You've come to say that a laptop doesn't cost two grand.'

I just stared at him. I didn't know if this directness was dangerous. The Provos had used boys younger than him through the years, after all.

'Look in the grate,' the washing machine woman said.

I looked over at her and she pointed at the fireplace. I took another step forward. There was no fire, but instead a pile of scrunched up paper, ripped cheques, in the cold grate.

'He gets through a book a week,' she said. 'There's no harm in it.'

I shook my head. Pinky scraped his chair round and, for an awful moment, I thought he was going to grab at my arm. He didn't, it was only to give him space to tell his story.

'Hugh Henderson,' he said, 'used to build houses, right? Up until the crash. Did a lot for the local economy and that. But then—' he brought his fists together, then apart with fingers splayed. 'It all went kaput. And she went and left him too.'

'His wife?' I asked.

'No, she left long ago. His daughter.'

'Dear love him,' the washing machine woman said.

Pinky turned his seat back to the table, satisfied that everything had been explained. I stood for a second more, took a final look at the piled cheques in the grate, and went back through to the main bar.

Hugh watched me all the way.

'So,' he said, with a wink, 'you've seen how things work. Buy me a drink and then tell me what you're after…'

He reached into his pocket for his chequebook. Behind the bar, the poured pint of *Guinness* was settling and the barmaid was already measuring out the whisky.

goosified (adj.):
affected with "goose-flesh"

When it was his turn to talk to Hayley, Murray stretched the phone cord until it could reach the hall cupboard. Then he spoke to his half-sister in a whisper, so that he wouldn't be heard by their mother.

'How's university?' he asked.

'Turns out the most complicated books have the least to say.' She paused. 'How's school?'

'Fine,' he said. 'Complicated.'

The wall of the cupboard held the chill of outside. Beyond it, Murray could hear the inhale-exhale of the waves and the clang of the ferry against the slipway; the ferry that brought Hayley home less-and-less often.

'Hayley,' he asked, 'is it right that when you fall in love your skin prickles and your hairs stand on end?'

There was silence, but only because she was thinking. She was good like that – never questioning his questions.

'I'm no expert,' she said, 'but I guess it is that. It's a mixture of excitement and fear, right enough, and it sends a chill through you but you're smiling at the same time.'

'Just that?'

'Like I say, I'm no expert.'

Murray was curious because of Sara. She lived in the flat above the pub. Their mums said the two of them were destined to get married – together they'd used the shells and stones on the beach as teething aids; the hill down from the kirk as a tandem-track; the seafront wall to swing their legs until the mortar showed the dent of where their heels hit.

Sara obviously had similar thoughts, because she'd asked Murray if he wanted to be her boyfriend. It was in full view of everyone, although he wasn't sure if they'd

34

overheard. He told her that he'd ponder it, and then wondered where that word had come from.

He liked Sara, no doubt. She had a curl to her dark hair and eyes that creased down to slats when she laughed. He felt a shiver when she sang Nina Simone, softly, on the walk to school and they would share a smile as they sent skimmer-stones out into the bay. But, love?

In the days that followed, Murray decided to experiment. He needed something for comparison, so he thought back to when he'd had goose-flesh in the past and then set about raising the pimples of it again.

First, he turned the radiator in the bathroom off and then the hot water on full. His right foot was near-numb as he lifted it into the bath. He held it there as it poached. He got his other foot in too, but then he had to run the cold tap. Next day he had a chilblain like a polished stone on his instep.

Cold to hot hadn't worked, so he tried the opposite. Bundled up in all the jerseys and coats he owned, he walked, sweat-slick, to the shore. It was only ten paces from his front door. He stripped to his boxers and splashed into the foam until he was in up to his shoulders. It knocked the breath from him and sharpened the pain at his ankle until it was as keen as a knife-wound. He gasped his way back out.

That night, in bed, he read the book Hayley had given him for his birthday. He remembered feeling something when he turned the final page; a wash of elation that had also brought tears to his eyes. Re-reading the first twenty pages did nothing, though.

He decided to redouble his efforts. In the morning, he paced up into the fields above the village and found the one with the bull. There was certainly a tinge of fear as he held his hand out towards the electric fence. He paused, felt the bull's brown eyes on him. With the first touch, his hand snatched itself back. The second – held for longer – left him

35

on his backside in the bracken. Still, he felt nothing except his thumping heart.

That afternoon, he sat on his bed with his headphones on and listened to *Mississippi Goddam* at full volume. He thought of Sara, certainly, but also of Hayley, who'd given him the CD. With his eyes closed, he resolved to move the experiment on to its acid test.

The ferry took the last of the daylight with it and also, thankfully, the gusting rain. There were lights in most windows, but the brightest came from the pub. Those too young to be inside stood at the corner and listened for the belch of conversation and laughter that came whenever the door opened.

Sara stood on the fringes. Murray walked up to her and held out his hand. She took it and he half-pulled her to where the melted-butter of light on the pavement faded into shadow. He had to stoop slightly to bring his lips to hers.

There was a cheer behind them, an attempt at a whistle, but Murray felt no knives at his instep, no backside in the bracken. His heartbeat was neither thumping nor stone-skipping. She tasted of aniseed, faintly, and her lips were cracked and dry.

'Does this mean I'm your girlfriend?' she asked, and he shrugged and felt the itch of the chilblain on his ankle.

'How's university?' he asked Hayley, on the phone, the next day.

'I'm looking forward to coming home at Christmas.'

'Only three weeks,' he said.

The cupboard smelt of peat. It probably came from his mum's boots, kicked off against the side-wall. Murray tried to think whether Sara had a smell and wondered whether the aniseed taste had been a coincidence or if she would always hold that flavour.

'I was talking to Mum…' Hayley said, on the other end of the line. 'And asking her if you could come back down with me after the holidays. For a wee visit, you know, to see a show and visit the big shops.'

'Yes,' Murray felt as breathless as after his sea-swim. He closed his eyes. 'And?'

'She said she didn't see why not.' She paused. 'So how does that sound?'

Murray didn't answer for a moment. He was savouring the sensation.

historiaster (noun):

an inferior or mediocre historian

Listen, Victor always had a head start. His collection began with the shrapnel and flak he gathered from the fields, scraps of parachute silk and the twisted section of a landing gear. He had watched the dog-fights and often scooped up shell casings while they were still warm.

I came to the island long after the war, though. I started out, decades later, with ration cards and shelter permission tickets. It was only a hobby. But then I found a flight instructor, working out of Luqa, who gifted me a Sutton harness and an old-fashioned Gosport Tube; used for the trainer, behind, to speak to the pilot, in front.

By that time, Victor had scrabbled together enough memorabilia to establish the War in Malta Museum from a lock-up garage in Marsascala. I was one of his first visitors, along with a scattering of tourists.

'You, boy,' Victor called, hooking a finger at me.

I pointed to my chest, surprised to be singled out. He coughed deeply and managed to turn it into a nod.

'I hear you have a harness,' he said, eyes narrowed, 'and various other items which belong in this museum…'

'I like to collect, yes.'

'We accept donations,' he said.

'Is that so?'

He paused, keeping a cough in his throat by pressing his knuckles against his lips. He waved his other hand in the air, as if hurrying me along.

'Fine, fine,' he said, 'I'll give you one lira for it.'

'For the harness?'

'For the lot.'

I had only recently turned twenty, but I knew when I was being hustled. Especially since the price of entry to his museum was 50c. I shook my head, just once, and left his museum. I never set foot in it again, or the extended premises he moved into five years later to provide room for the Tiger Moth aircraft and the Bren gun that he'd bought (illegally) from somewhere.

Instead, I came to the realisation that there must be good money to be gleaned from the tourists visiting Victor's meagre museum. So I set out to establish the Malta Wartime Museum in a disused storehouse by the village square. The Sutton harness took pride of place, alongside a rudder bar from a shot-down Hurricane and an old starter trolley I'd rescued from Hal Far.

Within a week of opening, I had a letter from Victor with the words "cease and desist" across the top and various threats and exhortations. It said I was sure to fail anyway because his collection was superior and he could outbid me for any item that came on the market. I decided to prove him wrong by travelling to Italy to secure a scrapped wing from a CR42. Victor might have been able to pay more, but I moved quicker than him and people were more likely to warm to a youngster's smile than the coughing fit of a middle-aged man.

It was around this time, as well, that I arranged access to the air-raid shelter, carved from the soft limestone beneath the misraħ. I added to my collection with a Bofors anti-aircraft gun and a magnetic skid sweep that had been used out in the Grand Harbour. My museum now had items from the Army, Navy, and RAF – as well as occasional tours of the disused shelter – so all of the concierges at the Hotel Phoenicia agreed that it was the museum they would recommend to tourists.

Victor wasn't willing to concede, though. He showed up one day with a balding man who peered over the top of his sunglasses to write on a clipboard. They paid the Lm2 entry fee, so I couldn't protest as they wandered through the Malta Wartime Museum and made notes.

'Those steps,' Victor muttered, 'down to the shelter. That low-ceiling and the streak of damp down the wall. The sharp edges there. And is that torpedo definitely disarmed...?'

I thought he was bluffing, if truth be told, but a few days later there was a letter with the Health and Safety decision. In previous times, it could have been appealed through the British Admiralty, but now there was a Minister in Valletta who wouldn't budge. Even after a letter to the editor of the *Times* complaining of institutional favouritism towards the War in Malta Museum.

For four months of the summer, we were closed. The tourist season came and went while I scrabbled about to make the building safe and write out the correct safety procedures. It seemed unlikely that Victor had any of that in place either, but that didn't matter because he was still open and welcoming visitors. Since I'd closed, he'd acquired the crest of the 7th Mine Countermeasures Squadron and shingles to go along with his hacking cough.

In that period, though, I developed a skill for filling out forms. There was European money available for accessibility improvements and, suddenly, a route opened through to funding a purpose-built extension. When we reopened, we were in the ideal position to cater for the tourists from Sliema and St Julian's, from the hotels that began to proliferate all the way up the coast. We increased our entry fee to Lm5.

Victor's museum began to charge less and less. He sat in an armchair beside his Tiger Moth and tried to force tour buses to the door of the War in Malta Museum by sheer force of will. Those who did show up received more information about the Malta Wartime Museum – in the form of vitriol and bile – then they did about the museum they were actually visiting.

As the rumours about insolvency began to swirl, I decided the time was right to make my move. I couldn't bring myself to visit his museum, so I found his home address in the book and travelled down to Marsascala on a sunny Saturday. His house was little more than a shack; the corrugated iron roof looked like it was held together only by rust. I knocked on a door that rattled loosely in its frame.

'What do you want?' he said, as he opened the door.

'I have a proposition for you…'

'Is that so?' he squeaked the door open another inch or so. He had his shoulder half-turned away. 'You want to join forces, is that it?'

'I want to buy you out. The Tiger Moth, of course, but everything else too.'

Victor stared, coughed, then waved a hand.

'How much?' he spluttered. 'How much for the lot?'

'One lira,' I said, smiling.

There came a noise from Victor like the crunching of scrap metal in a compactor and he doubled over, with his hands on his knees. It was impossible to tell whether he was coughing or laughing; or, indeed, if his next movement would be to straighten up or to keel over right there on his doorstep.

impanate (verb):

to embody in bread

Alex

The pinch of cold air, from the door opening, told him that someone had come in. The girl's puffer-jacket dripped onto the tiles and a droplet hung from the small silver ring in her nose. Her hair – he would realise later – was blonde, but it looked closer to the brown of hawser rope when wet. She stood, with her eyes closed, and breathed in. When her eyes opened, she looked straight at him. Grey eyes framed by smeared mascara.

'Sorry,' she said, 'I love the smell of baking bread.'

'Nothing to apologise for, I'm a baker.'

Alex spent the next thirty seconds unpicking what he'd said. Had it made sense or did it just sound like two unconnected statements? He meant that, as a baker, he liked the smell too. That he took it as a compliment. Especially from such a beautiful girl. Should he say that?

'Here,' he said instead, taking a brown bag, wafting it through the air and then folding it closed. He held it out over the counter.

'What's this?' she frowned and Alex found that it changed the rhythm of his heartbeat.

'Stupid really,' he said. 'I was trying to bag the smell.'

'That's sweet,' she grinned, and Alex had to press his kneading-knuckles against his chest. It wasn't that he was fearful of a heart attack; only that he felt like he should be sitting down, like he should be giving himself time to adjust to the arrhythmia.

'It's the sourdough-rye that smells best,' he said, reaching to the shelf behind.

'No, I—'

'I insist, please. Free the house. I mean, on the house.'

She came in every Tuesday and Thursday without fail. She would buy one sourdough-rye loaf and walk out with her nose in the bag like a glue-sniffer. Two days a week, always when Alex was working. Yet it was two months before he did anything about it.

The simplest course of action, he knew, would be to ask her out. But he convinced himself that too much time had passed. He couldn't form the words – even to the empty shop. So, instead, he took a wooden spoon and used a breadknife to saw the head from the handle. Then he used a metal skewer to scratch a message into the soft curve of the spoon-head: "Tomorrow 7pm, Prince Regent".

The Regent was a gin-cocktail place further into North Laine. He would bake the spoon-message into her Thursday loaf and then wait for her on Friday evening.

Grand romantic gestures seem like a good idea right through until the crucial moment. As Alex was working the dough, he sang to himself; folding in the spoon-message, he found he had a wee tremble of excitement in his fingers; and as the loaf baked, he stood in the middle of the shop floor and breathed in the smell. Just as she had on that first day. Yet, as it cooled, he began to worry – what if she found it creepy? If it broke the teeth of her breadknife? He would lose his job if she complained.

By the time she came in, he'd convinced himself that he should come clean. Hand over the specially-baked loaf, yes, but also explain what was inside.

'It's a little bit different,' he managed to say, as he held it out to her. He could feel his cheeks soaring to the temperature of the ovens.

43

'Oh, exciting,' she said.

'Special, just for you.'

She smiled and took a deep sniff. 'Lovely,' she said. 'I'm Jess, by the way. I'm in so often, I feel I should introduce myself.'

'Alex,' he said, taking her bare hand. That first morning, she'd been wearing gloves.

'See you,' she said.

'Hope you like it!' he called after her.

Jess

Most of the week, Jess was in the School of Art studio working on her screen-prints. She wore an over-sized lilac shirt and yoga leggings. But on a Tuesday and Thursday morning, she pulled on jeans and a top that didn't need a sleeve-roll or tummy-tie, and wandered down to mind the till in the seafront gallery.

They had seven of her prints stocked, but she'd only ever sold one. It was hunger, then, that had led her into the bakery that first day. And gratitude for the free loaf saw her tearing at it with her fingers even though she knew it would make her stomach twist and groan and ache like an infant with colic. She wouldn't make that mistake again.

Jess kept going back to the bakery, though. She liked the guy with the flour-streaked beard and the thick rust-red hair. She liked that he wore a little blue cap, even though the hair tufted from the sides. She enjoyed the ritual of going in and the aroma of the bread she couldn't eat.

Part of it was superstition, maybe. She took the loaves only as far as Brighton Dome and she gave them, there, to the homeless lad huddled in the doorway. As soon as she started doing this, she found that her postcards and sketches started to sell. She could afford the extravagance of two charity loaves a week, if it bought her enough karma to shift her art.

The day she introduced herself to Alex, she walked – as normal – to the Dome, but she nearly carried on past her rough sleeper. James, he was called. He was all angles: Adam's apple as prominent as a beak; elbows sharp enough to tear his sleeping bag. It was this skeletal appearance which had led her to start feeding him.

She almost walked past him, though, because she was thinking about Alex. Those big hands, trying to be careful as he lifted pastries; that tendency to say something touchingly garbled, like a toddler before bed. Jess walked back to young James and gave him the brown bag. She smiled, to apologise for nearly forgetting, but said nothing.

For the rest of the day, Jess sat at the till and sketched out a stencil that would give the swirl of the sourdough-rye. She would print it in earthy-brown, rust-red, but would leave a dusting of white flour on top.

An American bought one of her framed prints, of a seagull. She was grateful, of course, but she had to hold herself back from saying that it was nothing – would be nothing – compared to the print she was planning. She couldn't wait to get back to her lilac shirt and silkscreen.

With a purposeful stride – the kind that only comes with the arrival of a fresh idea – she made for home. She had a fold of money in her pocket, for once, but she quickly forgot that she'd intended to buy her flatmate a special dinner. To celebrate and to thank her for covering the heating bill last month.

By the time she remembered about the shopping, she had to cut back through the Royal Pavilion Gardens. She was wondering if, maybe, she could ask Alex about gluten-free loaves. Now that she knew his name. The awkwardness of her previous purchases could be quickly brushed off, surely.

As she came out of the gardens, she heard her name, shouted, from behind. She looked over to one of the benches. James was standing with three others. He stood on the bench, showing her something she couldn't see. He held it like a police badge.

'Yes,' he shouted. 'See you tomorrow.'

Jess waved and turned, quickly, away. Once she started buying gluten-free bread, she would have no spare loaves for James. But maybe, now that she was earning, she could hand him some cash instead – so that he could buy more of whatever it was that caused him to lose long weekends and think that Tuesday followed Thursday.

jazzaphonic (adj.):

of a sound: resembling or characteristic of jazz music

In the night, after she's gone upstairs, the only sound is the slurp-suck of the dishwasher and I slip in my ear-buds to drown out the sound with Kamasi Washington's "Final Thought" which starts soft but soon layers up with drum and brass and I'm shuffling through to the hall to check the shoulder-bag, again, even though I know it has everything we need – jelly babies (*Bassetts*), nappies (*Pampers*), nightdresses (*M&S*), babygros (ditto), lip salve (*Nivea*) and CDs (indie-shite) – then I flick open her purse to check that she has cash although, of course, she always has cash and she's had this bag packed for a week and the only thing that worries her – she says – is that I might lift something out of it when I'm fussing – as if – and with that thought I pull my hands away and, hooked in my fingers, is a wee cloth cap.

In the kitchen is the bottle of *Glenmorangie Lasanta* waiting, waiting for the celebratory dram – maybe today, maybe tomorrow – once we're done with the waiting, yes, when I can do more than lift the cork and sniff the sherry-cask finish – is it finish, I mean? – that will wet the head but which, I know, would also tuck me in tight tonight, if only there wasn't the chance of being flung from sleep – by screams, by panting, by a patient hand on the arm? – and having to take off, then, to the hospital with the taste of the whisky sharper than the taste of toothpaste and the frantic, frantic worry that I might be over the drink-drive limit, just maybe, with the strength of the stuff, never mind the guilt of the fact I'd been keeping it, saving it – like superstition, or karma, or a charm – like a test.

The front door is bolted – of course it is – but I peer through the glass at our *Punto* and I plan, plan, plan – even though it's been planned: there's de-icing spray in the glove-box and a blanket in the boot and a full tank of petrol;

the tyres are pumped and there's a shrapnel of coins to park with; the car-seat is in place – it has its own wee blanket over the top, so small, and that's petrifying, petrifying – and I try not to think of my friend Ben whose partner went in for a C-Section and he was left in a box-room to pace, pace, pace, and all he could hear was the tick-tock clock with the second-hand that punched forward and then bounced back, staying shudderingly still, and he didn't know if the wee one would ever get out of there – of that operating theatre.

She's upstairs, the only sound is the slurp-suck and I slip in the sound which starts soft but soon layers up and I'm shuffling through to the shoulder-bag – *Bassetts, nappies, M&S, M&S*, salve, indie-shite – then her purse to check cash, she always has cash, and the thing that worries her – she says – is when I'm fussing – as if – in my fingers, a wee cloth cap.

The kitchen bottle of *Lasanta* waiting, waiting – today, tomorrow – yes, lift the cork and the sherry-cask finish – wet the head, tuck me in tight tonight, flung from sleep – screams, panting, hand on the arm? – and take off, with the taste sharper than toothpaste and the frantic, frantic over the drink-drive limit, maybe, with the strength of the stuff, the guilt I'd been keeping – superstition, karma, charm – a test.

Door is bolted – of course – our *Punto* plan, plan – planned: de-icing spray and blanket in boot and full tank of petrol; tyres pumped and shrapnel to park; car-seat in place – wee blanket, petrifying, petrifying – Ben left in a box-room to pace, pace, and the tick-tock clock punched forward then bounced, shudderingly still, and he didn't know if the wee one – that operating theatre.

The slurp-suck and the sound which starts soft, shuffling shoulder-bag – *M&S, M&S* – then cash, cash, and worries – she says – fussing – as if – wee cloth cap.

Lasanta waiting – today, tomorrow – yes, the sherry-cask – tuck me in, flung from sleep – screams? – take off, the taste sharper than toothpaste, frantic, maybe, the guilt – karma, charm – a test.

Bolted – course – our *Punto* plan: blanket and petrol; pumped and park; car-seat– blanket, petrifying, petrifying – Ben left to pace, clock bounced, shudderingly, and the wee one – that operating theatre.

Slurp-suck, shoulder-bag – *M&S, M&S* – then cash, cash, worries – she says – cloth cap.

Lasanta – today, tomorrow – yes – tuck me in – taste sharper than toothpaste, maybe – charm – test.

Plan: blanket and petrol; pumped and park; car-seat – petrifying – pace, shudderingly, and – that operating theatre.

Shoulder-bag – *M&S* – cash, cash – cap.

Today, tomorrow – yes – taste sharper – test.

Petrol; park – pace – that operating theatre.

Cash, cash – cap. Yes – taste – test. Petrol; park – pace.

Cash – cap. Taste – test. Park – pace.

Cash – cap. Taste – test. Park – pace.

I take the ear-buds out and go upstairs. I lie down next to her and try to match the measured rhythm of her breathing. She doesn't turn. It is difficult for her, propped up as she is by pillows.

'What have you been doing?' she whispers, with the slur of sleep.

'Nothing.'

'You've been checking the bag again.'

I wait a beat. 'Yes.'

49

'Try to sleep.'

'What if we've forgotten something?'

'We'll improvise,' she says. 'Make it up as we go along.'

keckish (adj.):

inclined to keck; squeamish

Two weeks after dropping out, Langston took the train home for mid-semester break. He hadn't yet decided if he'd tell his parents, but he certainly held it back from his younger brother, Ted, who picked him up from the station and drove him back through the glen.

'You lucky shit,' Langston said, after a silence.

Ted didn't take his eyes from the single-track road. 'Eh?'

'Dad bought you this car, didn't he?'

There was a gear change, but no answer.

'He never gave *me* a car,' Langston said. 'Never.'

'You can't drive, Langy.'

'I would if I had a fucking car.'

'Besides, he sends you money every month.'

'That's for my studies, Ted.'

This was the aspect of leaving university Langston was still undecided about: whether to feel guilty about the money. Five hundred pounds a month into his account, so that he didn't have to distract himself with part-time work. His dad would have been so much more than an administrator if he'd been able to concentrate on his studies.

Langston had tried at medical school, he really had. Much of phase one was fine. He still retained information well and he'd always been excellent under exam-pressure. But he struggled with the guts and gore. In lectures, a slide showing a haematoma left him light-headed; then, on the A&E visit, the sight of a simple contact rash had him reaching out for the nearest chair. He had to spit out bile after being shown an infected surgical wound and then he fainted clean away at the blood donation truck.

Back at the house, his mum had put on a spread with

cold chicken and salad. She greeted him as 'Doctor' and he did nothing but smile back. Then, over a glass of wine, he told them about his semester. Yes, he said, he found the studying difficult but the hands-on aspect was absorbing. Why did he say that? Then, after half a glass, he managed to grip at the tablecloth and tell them about the cadavers, laid out on trestle tables for dissection. The heads were kept in a bucket underneath, ready for the dental students. He'd never actually seen these decapitated bodies, of course, but he'd been told what to expect in the next teaching block. He'd thought of little else since.

'Not lunchtime conversation, maybe,' his mum said, saving him from himself.

'Nonsense,' his dad replied. 'It's fascinating. And good for Teddy's schooling too.'

Ted glowered and tore at a chicken leg with his teeth.

The school had been very keen on Langston applying for Medicine. Not many did, around here, and his grades were certainly good enough. They'd had two going off to do Veterinarian Studies in recent years, but no doctors.

In his final year at school – the year Ted was in now – Langston had gone on a class visit to the Royal College of Surgeons in Edinburgh and left a green puddle on the immaculate marble floor. It was during a live-feed of a liver transplant, but Langston hadn't seen past the first incision. He told the teachers that he had a stomach bug.

'I've heard that you have to clamp the rib-cage open,' his dad said, waving a carrot-baton. 'Is that right?'

Langston took a breath through his teeth. 'I guess so.'

'You're at the coal-face, Langston, I've only ever been at the top of the shaft.'

'Really!' his mum looked shocked. 'Less of that!'

'There was no—'

'We're eating lunch, no more of it.'

52

That afternoon, they went for a walk to the loch. Langston trailed behind with Ted. He had to watch his footing; it had been a while since he'd worn wellies or negotiated the squelch of the boggy fields. The cows watched his every move, chewing slowly.

'It's fucking difficult, you know,' Ted said, suddenly.

Langston looked up. 'What is?'

'Following in your footsteps.'

Langston studied the brown-tipped toes of his wellies, even though he knew his brother wasn't speaking literally.

'With Mum and Dad, you mean?' he asked.

'And the school,' Ted was staring at him. 'No-one can say our fucking surname without attaching your exam results to it.'

'They're just proud.'

'Not of me.'

Langston pressed his toe into the mud until the ground belched. He knew that this was the moment he should tell his brother. Relieve the pressure, the expectation. *Ted,* he'd say, *you might think you've got a lot to live up to but, truth is, I can't so much as look at a toddler's grazed knee without passing out.*

'Ted,' he said, instead, 'sometimes it just takes time. To find what you're good at.'

'You've always known though, haven't you?'

There it was: the second opportunity to come clean. Again, Langston passed it up.

'You'll figure it out,' he said, and placed a hand on his brother's shoulder. He looked ahead to where their dad was waving an arm to hurry them along. Lengthening his stride, he moved away from Ted.

First, he felt the cold chicken in his stomach give a churn and bind, until it began to writhe like a foetus; then came the acidic burn in his throat that he'd felt when the consultant had drained that wound; and the mist behind his eyes that had drifted in when they'd talked of cauterisation and surgical amputation. That flush-chill from his reading about venereal disease.

Each step slipped back a little and his arms flailed. Still he stumbled on. He heard Ted's call from behind, and he half-twisted. In that moment, he fully intended shouting out. *Not to worry*, he'd cry, *I'm a fuck-up – I can write an essay, but I can't stitch a wound or even say the word "pustule"*.

His toe caught or his balance went or he blacked out for a moment, and over he went, face-first into the brackish water-mud of the field. Instead of lifting himself, he settled his cheek down into the filth of it and waited for Ted to catch-up.

leading-string (noun):

strings with which children used to be guided when learning to walk

They developed a system. Galina came up with it in those weeks after the last infection and those days, around Bill's anniversary, when Mia didn't rise from her chair.

'*H*en,' Galina said, with that guttural noise that sounded like phlegm. 'You *h*ave to eat, you *h*ave to move.'

She unfurled wool and cut it into lengths. One end was attached, with a small square of tape, to the wooden table beside Mia's armchair. The other end led to the things she'd need through the day: the cling-filmed sandwich on the kitchen counter; the TV pages over on the windowsill; the saucer of pills on the folded-down dining table. The wool was colour-coded: red for practicalities, blue for entertainment.

'I'm not senile,' Mia protested.

'Just a wee bit, lovely lady,' Galina said, and the first part sounded so snipped and Glaswegian and the second so rounded and foreign, that Mia forgot her anger.

Her son, Robert, usually came in the afternoon. When he first saw the wool stretched hither-and-yon, he made a comment about James Bond and laser tripwire, but he soon came to use the system too – red wool to her dinner in the microwave, blue to her book and nightdress on the adjustable bed in the dining room. The wool never continued up the stairs; Mia's legs weren't in a fit state for steps, so he'd put dust-sheets over everything up there and they now thought of the house as a bungalow.

Galina always came a little after eight, in the morning, and helped Mia to the bathroom. They changed the dressings on her legs – there was always seepage through the night – then Galina ran the hoover through the downstairs while Mia ate a slice of toast and drank a mug of milky coffee. Galina spent ten minutes hanging the strings. Then she went off to see to the rest of her "lovely hens" and Mia was left to unravel the wool of the next seven hours.

Robert arrived around four, after work and anxious to beat the traffic home. He worked in the IT department of a school and had never decided whether he should dress like the teachers or the kids. A shirt and tie would be paired with a zip-up hoody, jeans with formal shoes. Mia mentioned it daily.

By that time, Mia had usually followed all of Galina's strings to their ends. Robert would stretch them to their new destinations and then set her up with a DVD and a single *Highland Toffee*. The sweety never changed, but the films varied wildly depending on what was closest to the sliding doors in Robert's local library. Mia liked the type of film with jokes based on chaos and misunderstanding, but she tended to get ones with titles about wives or notebooks, and often ones with black-and-white scenes in concentration camps.

Halfway through her film, after Robert had left, Mia would go and heat her dinner. While it cooled, she changed into her nightdress. She carefully wound the lengths of wool and placed them into her pocket. She insisted that Robert buy her nightdresses with pockets.

When the streetlights came on, Mia raised herself from the armchair and turned off the film-credits. She twitched the curtains closed. Robert thought that the next part of her routine was going to bed with a book. He would have been horrified to know the truth.

Going upstairs took her an age. She shuffled up sideways, both hands on the bannister. Beneath her dressings, the scabbed skin on her legs cracked and ruptured, but she felt it only as warmth. The pain would come later. And, tomorrow,

Galina would again despair at the inability of Mia's skin to fuse, to knit, to heal.

At the top, Mia placed her forehead against the cool of the wall and waited for her breathing to slow. It was now that the pain crept in. She kept her eyes closed. Then, when she was ready, she opened her eyes and looked over to her bedroom. There was a cat's cradle of blue and red wool pulled over every available surface, under the plastic sheeting and tight across the mid-air between dresser and bed.

Red was for Robert, blue for Galina. Long ago, she'd tied a length of blue to each of the rings in her jewellery box but she now remembered that there was also a bracelet in the second drawer of her dresser. It would look good on Galina's slender wrist. And in the spare room, across the hall, was the framed lino-print that Bill had made her for their silver wedding anniversary. Robert should have that.

It wasn't always as simple as trailing the wool out to the hallway where she'd written her instructions, in black felt-tip, halfway up the magnolia wall. Sometimes the paths – into the bathroom and the boxroom that still held Bill's binders of sketches – meant that she needed to tie two or three lengths end-to-end. The reused squares of Sellotape often didn't stick either. When that happened, Mia took her square of toffee, wetted it under the tap, and kneaded until it formed a sticky putty.

She didn't want the threads to run straight. The whole idea was that it would take the two of them some time. The red that led to the folder of deeds in the boxroom and the blue that was tied to the carriage clock in the spare room intersected. The blue from one album of photographs, in the bedroom, was tangled with the red of the album that sat next to it, but the knots and snarls of it would have to be unpicked in the hallway. They would have to spend time, side-by-side, those two who usually arrived at different ends of the day.

After she'd finished laying the wool, Mia stood for a moment in the hallway. It was like standing in the middle of a loom. Threads ran towards her, away from her; disappeared under rugs, reappeared from behind the wardrobe. Each and every one of them ended on that magnolia wall, where small squares of Sellotape and great globs of toffee stuck them next to the words "Robert is red, Galina is blue".

Every night, before she made her slow descent, Mia would finish the Valentine's rhyme. 'Time for grandkids, you two,' she'd say. Or, 'Sit my ashes in the front pew.' She always said it just loud enough that her voice would carry through to the boxroom. And every night she thought she heard that cackle of laughter, that rustle of papers, that sound of her Bill scraping his chair back and finally coming to bed.

mizzle-shinned (adj.):

having one's legs red and blotched from sitting too near a fire

Greg has grown up too quickly: two kids and the type of mortgage that has you counting copper coins. Whereas Andy is still essentially a teenager: shifts in a supermarket in the day, then eccies to see him through the nights out. The three of us meet once a month, on a Wednesday evening, to catch up.

I like to think I've charted a middle ground: one kid, no mortgage, a pint or two on the weekend. That said, it's me complaining about the call-centre that gets us on to the subject of our worst ever job.

'For me,' Greg says, 'it was the call-centres. Sorry, pal. Not like yours, though; this was cold calling and I was right at the bottom of the pyramid.'

'What pyramid?'

'Promotion and that, you know.'

He's a Loss Adjuster now, is Greg, which should mean that he's able to budget well-enough to buy a round, but it's still always myself or Andy who end up getting them in.

'Mine was that chip shop,' I say. 'Just the grease of it, eh. And the embarrassment when the girls from school came in and I was standing there in a wee white apron and hat.'

'Did you not give them free chips, no?'

'Boss wouldn't let me. They'd have been out my pay.'

'Tight-arse.'

I look at Greg, then at the pint Andy bought me. Over the months, it's been at least a dozen rounds since Greg reached for his wallet. The moths in there must have fossilized by now.

'What about you, Andy?' Greg asks.

'Eh?' Andy blinks, re-focuses.

'Your worst ever job?'

Andy chews at his lip. He scrapes his fingernails over his stubble and it makes a noise like a match being struck.

'Well...' he says. 'Probably that week or so I spent as assistant to an alchemist.'

I look at Greg, Greg looks at me. We burst out laughing. In that moment, I can see a glimpse of the young lad who used to play chappy on all the neighbourhood doors. Then he shakes his head, puts on his dad-voice.

'Andy, I think you might mean chemist. Or pharmacist, maybe.'

'Do I, aye?' Andy looks confused. Looking across at him, I raise my eyebrows. I don't want to come across as patronising or that. Don't want to give the impression that I think Andy's brain is addled, that his memory's only just this side of fucked.

'Tell us about it,' I say. 'Then we can work it out.'

'Right,' he gulps at his pint before starting. 'It was a wee card in the window of a newsagent that led me to it – red with gold lettering – and the house was one of them grand ones in the West End. It had this wee tower on the side of it.'

'Sounds like one of the kids' fairytales,' Greg says.

'Aye, so, the house was all overgrown and that; peeling paint, weeds out the gutters. And the door is opened by this man wearing a tweed suit and with grey hair that was thin as cobwebs in some places and thick as a duvet in others. Mental-looking fella, with wee sunken eyes that stared right through you...

'So, I tell him why I'm there and he takes me through corridor after corridor. Then, on the landing, there's like a zoo's worth of stuffed animals – they're all staring at me as well.'

'Taxidermied,' Greg says, taking a sip.

60

'Aye, but he tells me to pay them no mind and leads me on to this wee spiral staircase. And, honest to god, there's a baboon on one side and this wolf-thing on the other, like they're guarding it. So we climb up these stairs and through a hatch into this tower-room. There are shelves all around the walls, with books on half of them and jars filled with powders and herbs on the rest. Then, right in the middle of the room, is this massive fire-pit. Flames are leaping out of it, the rim's only one brick high. And hanging over it, from a chain, is this giant metal disc, like one side of a set of scales.'

'Fucking hell,' I breathe. 'It doesn't sound like a pharmacy anyway.'

'He's at the wind-up,' Greg says.

It takes Andy a moment before he shrugs at Greg, but it takes him a beat before he does anything these days. If this is a wind-up, he's been working on his poker-face for the best part of a decade now.

'So what happened?' I ask.

'This fella – Dr Vata, he's called – takes a wee bit of metal, looks like the hinge off a door, and throws it onto the disc above the fire. And it goes like molted-hot and all this smoke starts coming off it…'

'Molten,' Greg corrects him.

'… and when the smoke clears there's this glow to the metal, but not heat.'

'Was it gold then?' I ask.

'He said it was, aye.'

Greg scoffs. He swirls his pint glass. 'Fuck sake,' he says.

'But I only stayed about a week,' Andy says.

'Why did you leave?' I ask.

Andy scrapes his chair back and pulls up the left leg of his jeans. He tugs his sock down to his tattered trainer. On his ankle are several silver flecks that catch the light. They're scar tissue, the size of fingernail clippings.

'Couldn't take the heat of that bastard-fire,' he says.

I look up into Andy's face. It's like he's showing us where he fell off his bike or from a swing. Greg leans across.

'Bull*shit*,' he says. 'It's from a Scout bonfire or sitting too close to your nan's electric heater. Bull*shit*.' Then he swallows the rest of his pint and stands. 'I'm away to the bog.'

Andy folds down his jeans. 'Get a round on the way back then. I'm beginning to think that wife of yours has your pockets sewn-up.'

Greg looks back with his mouth open, but the best he can come out with is, 'You're the one who has a mate who can turn metal into gold.'

For a minute, we sit in silence. Andy is looking over my shoulder, at a TV screen with football news on it. He sniffs, but seems unaware that I'm staring at him. When he does look my way, he seems surprised.

'What's up with you?' he says.

'Was all that for real?' I ask.

'All what?'

'The alchemy stuff.'

'Aye,' he blinks. 'I knew that fucker wouldn't believe me, though.'

'Then why didn't you go back?'

'Eh?'

'Why didn't you go back to the alchemist's house, if he was making gold?'

Andy shrugs. 'It wasn't for me.'

I smile and sit back in my seat. 'Greg's right, you're full of shite.'

Andy keeps his eyes on the TV, but he reaches into his pocket and pulls out his wallet. From the fold behind the notes, he pulls out something the size of a door-hinge. He places it on the table between us and I lean forward. It catches the light in the right way; it's the right colour.

'I might still have that wee red-and-gold card,' Andy says, 'if you're not precious about your ankles…'

notaphily (noun):

the study or collection of banknotes

They got away with twenty-six million, but I only seen about ten grand of that and, even then, it was them useless recalled notes, the ones with the old design on them. One of the boys – I'll not be telling you who, now – gave me this stack of them and I says to him, 'What would I be wanting these for?' and he shrugs and says, 'You can use them to wipe your arse, missus, for all I care.' They knew the serial numbers of those notes, you see, the security services and that, so I may as well have been holding a pile of bog-roll.

All the same, I put them away in shoe boxes and slid them in under our Kieran's bed. I wasn't for behaving like some of the other ones; lifted at the corner shop for trying to pass off a stolen twenty or questioned by the peelers for buying some Bulgarian timeshare. No, I decided that I'd as soon sit on that worthless money and see whether it might ever get itself a bit of worth again.

There's stories in the papers about the job, right enough. They're saying it might have been an inside man, at the bank, or even the old Special Branch of the Royal Ulster Constabulary on the take for one final time. Truth be told, they don't have a notion. All they know is that two of the ones with keys for the vault had their families taken hostage. The usual thing: gunmen in balaclavas. Then, the next day, those same two men opened the doors and the safes so that the robbers could dander in without so much as a word of a challenge. Fair enough, if you're asking me. Why would you want to go risking the lives of your family for someone else's money. There's no call for it. The bank'll be insured and you're as well doing what the boys say so your family get released no bother. And they did as well, didn't they? Not a scratch on them.

Down the road, there's a wee lad called Declan – known to our Kieran – who got spooked when he was given his pile of useless notes. The eejit that he is, he builds himself a bonfire in his back yard and starts putting armfuls on. Thousands of pounds. And one of his neighbours sees the lit notes drifting on the breeze and, soon enough, the whole place is surrounded. There's no link between him and the robbery itself, though, so all they can get him for is the handgun they find up the stairs and membership of the Provisional IRA.

That gets me worried, a fair bit, about our Kieran. After all, they're more likely to blame the seventeen-year-old hallion than the forty-year-old housewife. So I move the shoe boxes from under his bed and put them out in the garage instead. Then I tell Kieran that it's time he was moving out and away from his mammy. Which is no word of a lie, banknotes or no banknotes.

I hear tell, as well, of Niall – cousins with our Julie – who buried near enough twenty grand in his allotment. He put it in plastic *Tesco* bags, he says, but the wet got in anyway and he ended up with mulch. Still, he's well enough connected that he got handed another five grand and told to take better care of it.

Word around here is that they got too much. The robbers, I'm meaning. They were thinking that they'd find a couple of million in used notes, maybe some euros and dollars as well, and they could provide a wee hand-out for the gunmen left behind by the peace process. As it was, they found enough cash to buy half of Belfast and they got greedy and swiped the lot. Then the bank went and took the old-design notes out of circulation and we're left with Declan's bonfire, Niall's mulch and my shoeboxes.

And it's not until four years later that I have my idea. Kieran's out of the house, by then, and our Erin too. I'm reminded of the notes in the garage by the news that one of the bank-workers is to stand trial and then I'm in the bar down at the end of the street and there's this American tourist in and he's talking loud-as-you-like about the mural tour he's just been on and the money he's given, over the years, to be sent over the water for the "struggle". And it sets me thinking. So I go over to him and I says, 'Would you be wanting a wee memento of that there robbery?' And he does that shout-talking back, so I tell him to quiet down and stay there with his pint of *Guinness*. Then I go off home and take the picture of Kieran out of the black frame on the mantle and I get a ten-pound note from the shoe boxes in the garage. Back at the pub, I sell the framed note to your man for forty quid.

That's how it all starts. I put word out through the taxi drivers who're doing the tours and ask wee Dervla behind the bar to keep an eye out too. I'm thinking there must be a message board or newsletter for those American types as well, because soon enough there's a steady stream and I'm buying the wee frames in bulk. That's my only outlay, though, the rest is profit.

The lad from the bank is acquitted, later in the year, and the robbery isn't in the news so much, but I still have my customers. The most of them have American accents, but there's a few Scots and the odd German or Japanese. I've a thought or two about undercover officers, but it's unlikely they could charge me for much beyond handling stolen goods and some kind of fraud. I'd probably be out of the jail even before our Erin has the wee baby she's expecting. And, in the meantime, I've made near-enough twenty-five grand out of that ten grand of useless notes. It's money laundering, aye, but only like doing your delicates; careful, small-scale.

All the same, the shoe boxes are nearly empty and I'm fretting about that more than about a knock on the door. I

66

could go back to the boys that gave me it in the first place, but the ones with connections have long-since washed their hands of it. Or I could go to Niall – through our Julie – and see if he still has his second lot of notes.

In the end-up, though, I decide that I'll just start going to the cash machine and getting the notes with the new design. I'll still have a decent profit margin and those American tourists would buy a fag-end if you told them Bobby Sands had once smoked it. Besides, by the time they're on the other side of the Atlantic, it's not a bother if they realise that the banknote they've got framed on the wall is legal currency and not part of the robbery haul.

I'll only keep it up until I've got enough to get our Erin settled or until I get lifted; whichever comes first. If I get caught now, though, then it won't be for using notes from the robbery, it'll just be for scamming some dip-shit tourists with money lifted from the ATM. And no jury's going to do much about that beyond having a wee chuckle to themselves and maybe muttering, under their breath, 'Go on yourself, Rosemary, serves the stupid buggers right.'

ombrometer (noun):
a rain gauge

Tom watched his granny from the kitchen window. She rose higher on her right-step than her left. When they replaced her hip, they must have fitted her with the wrong size. She made her lopsided way to the centre of the sheep-grazed grass, where a copper cone was dug into the earth. Inside was a glass vial which gathered rainwater.

'Four-point-four millimetres,' she said into the phone, back in the kitchen, or 'twelve-point-six' or 'barely a millimetre today.'

Tom would look over the rim of the cereal box he was pretending to read and wonder who was on the other end of the line. Why did they care how much rain had fallen on that field? There would be a few words of small talk and then his granny would say goodbye and hang up.

For the rest of the day, while Tom was at school, his granny would be occupied by her embroidery. Over the years, the things that she stitched had been growing smaller and smaller. When Tom was really young, she made quilts that could be draped between two chairs as a tent. Then she'd downsized to cushion covers, barely big enough to use as Native American headdresses, before shrinking again, to napkins and handkerchiefs. She sat at the kitchen table, the beam from the lamp reflected in her thick glasses, working as quickly as her trembling hands would allow.

Then came a week when she couldn't get her thread through the eye of the needle. The doctor sent her to bed, so Tom had to heat her soup, peel her oranges and, in the morning, carefully carry the glass vial back from the field.

He thought that he'd finally have the chance to speak to the person on the other end of the line. Instead, though, his granny asked him to turn her radio down and stretch the upstairs phone across until the flex was a tight-rope between the chest of drawers and the bed. Then she coughed her measurement, listened for a moment, made a noise in her throat and hung up.

'Your grandmother's looked after you all these years,' the doctor said. 'Now it's your turn to look after her.'

His granny's turn had started three years ago, after the car crash. Tom didn't have many memories of his parents, but he could picture the way his mum's blonde hair drifted across her face when it was caught by the wind and he could hear the three ways his dad said "kiddo"; with his voice deep to tell Tom off, with a wee note of laughter, and with a soft whisper before bed. His mum hadn't called him "kiddo", but his granny said that she'd often call him "sweetheart" or "Tom-Tom". He couldn't remember that, though.

Tom did ask the doctor how long his turn would be, but all he got was a half-smile and a pat on the arm. Mrs Martin next door, though, told him that she'd deliver some shopping for them every Tuesday and Friday, to keep them stocked-up, and Tom's schoolteacher asked him to bring his dirty uniform by her home so that she could run it through the washing machine. So they muddled-through, as his granny would have said. And every morning, the flex was pulled on the upstairs phone and the measurement was croaked into the handset.

For weeks, Tom watched his granny take the vial, squint at the marks on the side of it, and take the phone from him. She always had to shift across the bed, raising a groan from the mattress, and then she would repeat the measurement to herself, with her lips moving, before lifting the receiver. It took a total of nine seconds, from the moment Tom handed her the phone.

In the school holidays, Tom decided it was time to listen in. After delivering the vial and stretching the flex across, he raced downstairs and lifted the handset in the kitchen. His timing was perfect. He placed his hand over the mouthpiece and listened as she dialled.

'Met Office,' a voice answered after three rings. It was a female voice. There was a pause, then Tom heard the side of the conversation he was used to: his granny giving her name and the measurement. There was the noise of a keyboard tapping, then a 'Thank you.' Tom heard the phone being put down upstairs. The line was silent for a few seconds.

'Hello?' the voice said.

'Hi.'

'Is that Tom?'

Tom nodded, then realised it couldn't be heard. 'Yes.'

'Ah, I thought so. How are you, sweetheart?'

He put the receiver down carefully, making sure that it didn't clatter or *ding*. His sobs were also quiet, held in his throat. He didn't even sniff, but instead wiped at the trail of snot and tears with his sleeve.

Every day, after that, Tom had a whispered conversation with the woman in the Met Office once his granny had hung up. She asked how his granny was keeping and what he was learning about in school. She told him that the rainfall was higher in the south of England that week than it was in Scotland, which was unusual. She said, 'Look after yourself, sweetheart,' before they said goodbye.

Tom never found out her name; which meant that he didn't know who to ask for on the day a male voice answered. It was all he could do not to blurt out the question while his granny was still on the line. He held it back, though, until he heard the phone being put down upstairs.

'Wait!' he hissed into the phone. 'Where is she today?'

'Hello,' the man said. 'Is this Tom then?'

'It is, yes.'

'We talk about you every day. It's nice to speak to you.'

'Is she ok?'

'She's fine, it's just my turn to talk to you if that's ok?'

Tom didn't answer.

'Are you managing ok?' the voice asked. 'Looking after your granny and all that?'

'We're muddling-through.'

'Glad to hear it.' There was a pause. 'Sounds like you're doing a great job, kiddo.'

philobiblian (noun):

a book-lover

We walked back via Kelvinbridge. This was the mid-Nineties so my team, Partick Thistle, were on another slide down the leagues. With red-and-yellow scarf up over my mouth, I practised my griping and grumbling about the game. I knew what it took to be a real fan. Like the man, in the seats behind us, who said 'I've seen enough of this' after ten minutes but then stayed until the end to join in with the boos.

My dad, walking beside me, paused by the turn-off to Otago Lane. I carried on for a step or two, dragging at his hand. This was another part of our Saturday routine: Dad wanting to stop off at every second-hand bookshop and record store on the way home and me, fidget-filled, chiding at him to pass them by. I began negotiations.

'Ten pence a minute.'

'A penny.'

'Five pence.'

'Two.'

'Fine, but I get to time it.'

He unbuckled his watch and handed it down to me. I started timing from the moment we left the main road. The shop was down a cobbled lane. The walls seemed to be made of books. Piles upon piles. There was no order to them, so searches needed to be carefully planned archaeological digs. Landslides were common.

There were no *Asterix* comics or *Just William* books. I'd checked. All the books seemed to have titles as complex and multi-layered as the stains on their spines. My dad picked them up, flicked through two or three pages, then set them back down.

After eleven minutes, I tapped at the watch in my hand.

72

I'd made twenty-two pence. He held up two fingers – two more minutes. By the time we actually left, I'd made another eight pence. Then I earned eighteen pence in the record store – where my dad pulled the black discs from their sleeves, inspected their ridges, then slipped them back onto the shelf – and another ten pence from a bookshop that had a cat curled on the counter; tabby fur against tarnished, mottled leather hardbacks.

My dad was in debt to the tune of fifty-eight pence by the time we made it home. I settled for a single shiny fifty pence coin and a promise that I could stay up for *Match of the Day*.

Two decades later, I'm in Brighton on a sunny Saturday. Partick Thistle are playing, but the best I can do is check the score on my mobile phone. We drink gin cocktails at a beachfront bar: me, my wife, and two friends. As clouds gather, we make our way up to North Laine. By that time, the final whistle has blown in Glasgow. Partick Thistle win at home for the first time this season, against Aberdeen. My dad is there and so too, presumably, are the "real fans" – who will mutter 'About bloody time' and turn towards the exits.

In the tight capillary streets of North Laine, I hold two fingers up to my wife – two minutes – then veer off into a bookshop. There are electronic security detectors at the door, but I don't think the pencil marks inside the covers of the books would set them off. I browse quickly, aware that the others are waiting. There is a book of stories by Deborah Levy that I'd like and a novel by Jon McGregor. Then I come across a book by Ronan Bennett. I loved his *The Catastrophist*, so I pull this book off the shelf too. I have three now. Each has a pencil-scribbled £3 inside, the pound-sign looking like a reflection of the number. I only have seven pounds and change, though, so I'm faced with a dilemma. This isn't the type of place that accepts cards.

I don't know how many minutes pass before my wife comes to find me and turns my left wrist with gentle fingers until my watch is facing upwards.

'The others are waiting,' she says.

'I have three.'

'That's ok,' she smiles. 'You can have three.'

'I don't have enough.'

'Do you want some money?'

I nod.

For the rest of the evening, I sit with a brown paper parcel of books beside me. With the arrival of each new drink, I remind myself not to forget them. By the fifth or sixth, neurosis takes over and I borrow a pen from the barman so that I can scrawl my address on the package – just in case.

On the train back home, I keep my arms crossed over them. We debate the Scottish Independence Referendum with a drunk from Hastings who tells me that I'd have to be certifiable to vote Yes, but then confides that, if he were Scottish, he would definitely vote for independence. I point out the contradiction, so he repeats his argument. The same words but louder.

To give myself an excuse for ignoring him, I peel open my parcel and flick through the first few pages of each of my second-hand books. There is a coffee-stain on the second page of the McGregor novel.

When I get home, I will phone my dad. He will tell me about the match and I will tell him about the books I bought this afternoon. It will cost nine pence per minute.

queuemanship (noun):

the exercise of ploys and tactics in order to minimize time spent waiting in a queue

You see folk lined up by the side of the bank building on Blythswood Street, some of them just standing but others with wee camping chairs or sleeping bags to lay out on the pavement. So you go up to the group at the back, three young lassies, and you wait for a gap in their conversation so you can ask what they're waiting for. Only there is no gap – they gulp in breaths only when they drop a t or miss an h – so you never get the chance. Maybe if you hadn't had a drink – if you weren't keeping down a belch, holding back from swaying – then you'd interrupt, but as it is the moment passes. There are two or three others behind you now, more arriving, and you're part of the queue.

No harm in that, you decide. It's a summer's night – not warm but not baltic either – and you've not got work in the morning. Stay for a while, see where this all leads. From the next street comes a throb of bass and there's a wee cheer that drifts around the corner too. So there's bound to be something worthwhile at the front: concert or footy tickets, the latest gadget or phone, some massive discount on a telly or holiday or car or whatever. You've only got that pittance left on your credit card, right enough, but if it's something you can turn a profit on then it'll be worth the wait.

The smart thing to do, you realise, would be to step out of line and go onto Sauchiehall Street, to see what shop or sign-up sheet or superstar is at the end of it all, but there's already a couple of dozen behind you and so it becomes vital that you don't lose your place. Stay in the game until you reach the corner, at least.

In front, the three girls are looking at something on a phone so you reach out a hand to the man beyond, as if you

75

know him, and step around them. You clap the man on the shoulder, smiling as he frowns, and then muttering that you thought he was someone else. By that time, though, you're next to him and the three girls are left behind.

You stay there for a couple of minutes, not wanting to draw attention to yourself, but there's a hip-flask doing the rounds a wee bit further on and you like the look of that group – young students with checked shirts and piercings – so you take a cigarette from your pocket and you stretch through to ask them for a light. A wee nod and a shrug to the folk you're stepping past, then offer the cigarettes around the students. Three of them take one and you take a swallow of their whisky in return, and you've jumped another couple of places in the queue.

It should be a given that they're talking about whatever it is they're waiting for, but two of them are on about coursework and the rest are listening to this sob-story about how someone called Andrea broke up with someone called Carl. And you have this wee panic, then, that this might all be a big mistake – this might be the queue for a taxi-rank or to get into a club. You don't need a taxi to get home – the distance isn't worth the fare – and you've not been in a club since your second kid was born.

The corner is close now, though, and you spot a cash machine in the wall which gives you the chance to elbow through. Take out forty, in case it's needed, and then nestle back into line. Up in front, there's a small stooshie about someone cutting in, so you reach forward and take a fistful of their jacket so you can join in with throwing them out of the queue and, at the same time, bring yourself forward that little bit more.

Then, just like that, you're round the corner. You look at the faces around you. There's excitement on them, right enough. And you're feeling it too, because there's big spotlights strobing the sky ahead and this fire-eater waving a flaming torch. He swallows the flame, big flourish, and everyone more-or-less ignores him; their eyes fixed to the front. Yours are too, but you can't see the sign of the shop at the end.

You pretend to stumble, taking you past the couple in front. There's a wee shout of protest, but it doesn't matter because you've caught sight of the sign – *Taco King* – so you can step back in line and—

Fucking tacos? What in the hell are tacos, even? You'd say it's the ones with the hard shells, because the soft shells are burritos, but there's no difference with the tomato-mince mix, is there? Or is it to do with the extras you get – the guacamole, the jalapenos, the beans, the cheese? Before you met the missus you wouldn't have even known what guacamole was but, even with her influence, you've still never had a taco in your life. Not once. And you're about to barrel out of the queue and make for home because you know Karen will give you pelters for being even this late and the wee one has ballet in the morning. Then again, you've never had a taco in your life. Not once. And you've come this far.

So you stay. In line, in your place. Ten minutes more, maybe fifteen, and when you reach the rush of warmth and light at the counter you smile at the young lad on the other side and you breathe deep – salt and frying fat and maybe just the hint of a mouth-watering onion – and you find yourself ordering ten of them. Ten tacos. That seems right. And the young lad doesn't blink, only asks if you want a drink, and you nod and wish you could order more than a coke.

Outside, to the side of the queue, you unwrap the first and it's the size of the palm of your hand, no bigger, and limp as a lettuce leaf. Maybe ten wasn't too many, after all, and maybe the soft shell isn't a burrito.

Three bites is all it takes, and then you eat a second in four bites. Pause for a slurp of coke, then the third in six bites. You're running out of steam now. You should take the rest home for Karen, for the kids, but why would they want seven tacos? Knowing Karen, she'll have tried the bastard-things before anyway and she'll not be keen on the wee one having hers reheated for a breakfast before ballet.

Looking about yourself, you go back to the corner and look back up Blythswood Street. The queue still goes back up a fair way. You don't want to join it at the end, but you'd fancy being back in the middle of it, feeling that anticipation and sharing the moment with those around you. So you pick a group of three lads – nervous to be out so late, not old enough to be chancing their arm trying to get into bars – and you move across to them. You open the brown bag and show them the tacos – two for each of them, one for yourself – on the basis that you can cut in line, that you can wait with them for a minute. Only for a minute, mind, because the corner's coming up soon enough and as soon as you've caught sight of those spotlights, of that fire-eater, of the folk entering with nothing and leaving with those brown bags, then you'll be off home to Karen and the kids.

rodges-blast (noun):

a sudden small, localized whirlwind

It rose up to mark the spot where she'd buried him. Or what remained of him. A swirl of leaves, at first, no more than would be lifted by a breeze; but then enough to raise the stony top-soil and scatter it out beyond the fence that lined the field.

Jenny watched from the kitchen window, hands in the cooling dishwater, and wondered why passers-by weren't rushing out, pointing and videoing it on their phones. Why weren't there camera-crews, for that matter, with reporters setting up on the pavement, or thrill-seekers seeing how close they could get without their feet being whipped out from underneath them?

She did venture out, because she needed to see whether it had stripped away too much and exposed his shallow grave. And, as she got closer, she saw that it wasn't directly over the spot but was, instead, circling slightly, moving up to the coarse grass at the side and bending the branches of the trees in the next field over. She stood still, waiting for it to come to her. When it did, it birled her around like a drunken dance-partner and left her on her knees several yards away with tears in her eyes and a stinging graze on the palm of her hand.

The next day Jenny went out again and it tore at her unwashed hair and dragged her cardigan from her shoulders. But she managed to stay upright.

Even if someone were to get curious about the whirlwind – now five days old and above the height of the trees – they'd have no reason to connect it with her husband; no call to begin asking questions. She'd been careful, after all: deleting her search history after those evenings looking up the most efficient way; travelling all the way out to Hallglen to buy the necessary from that lad. He had a scar, in place of a dimple, that deepened as he frowned. He looked the part and Jenny didn't, she knew that.

These should have been the first days of her freedom: she could visit that wee tea-room with the dainty china cups; she could take a walk to the Abbey and then carry on along the river. She could leave her watch at home. As it was, though, she stood and stared out of that window. She pulled at the stitching of her cardigan until it was as loose as a fishing net and, when the rain came, she watched the droplets catch in the wind and spin like a shoal of silver fish.

He was a good man, she told herself, even though that hadn't been true by the end. She said it aloud, looking over at his empty armchair, but it was only the cat who gazed back.

After a week, she invited her sister and one of the neighbours over for afternoon tea. The whirlwind was clearly visible from the sofa, out of the long window at the side, but neither of them passed comment.

'He was a good man,' she told them.

'Not by the end,' her sister replied.

'This summer would have been our fortieth wedding anniversary.'

Jenny didn't know why she'd said that; they hadn't celebrated since their thirty-second. She sipped her tea and tried to avoid looking out of the window.

'Still,' the neighbour said, 'there must be a part of you that's mighty relieved. Forgive me for saying so.'

'Aye,' her sister said, 'there's no shame in thinking of it as a burden lifted.'

Jenny didn't say anything. She was wondering how they hadn't yet seen the whirlwind. It had gathered enough stones, soil, leaves and plastic packaging to look something close to solid now; the grey cone of it cast a shadow when the sun was behind.

'It was an awful disease,' her sister said.

'Dreadful,' said the neighbour.

'And you were a saint, Jenny.'

He'd been very ill, it was true. Jenny had cared for him for the best part of a decade. She'd used his armchair as an auxiliary nurse, to hold him while she got him dressed, and the radio as a companion, so that his murmurs and groans weren't her only conversation. There'd been actual nurses, towards the end, and her sister had been a great comfort, of course.

The online searches had started as her looking for ways to ease the pain. Heroin isn't so very different from the morphine he was prescribed, and you can get it in Hallglen. Not too much, but enough for a peaceful transition. It had taken some nerve, but then she'd only had to make a phone call. She'd feared a spiralling – a wee glance from the doctor, a call to the police, nights in a cell, court-dates, a front-page splash, folk lined up to spit at her in the street – but none of that had come. She'd had him cremated and ashes were in a tin-urn out beneath the whirlwind.

After they'd finished their tea, Jenny took her sister and neighbour out to the fence that led to the field. They couldn't fail to see it from there. The three women stood, in a row, looking out across the flat expanse of the carse, with the Ochil mountains in the background and the Wallace Monument perched up on the hillside to their left. Jenny waited for the whirlwind to circle round to them. She closed her eyes as she felt the first gust of it, leaning into it slightly. It twisted her and she had to take a step to brace herself, but it passed in a matter of moments. She opened her eyes and looked over to her sister. The wind had brought tears to her eyes as well, and she'd reached out to hold onto the fence-post. Jenny turned to see what her neighbour made of it, but she was already lumbering away back to her own house, muttering that the washing would need to come in from the line if there was a storm brewing.

scraw (verb):

to clear the throat, to "hawk"

We invented the game together. Floating islands, it was called. We'd kneel on the wooden bridge over the burn and hack-cough. Then we'd nod to each other and let the spit trail from our lips down to the water. First island to come out the other side won. Jack's were always thick but slow-moving. Mine were fast but tended to split apart. That was automatic disqualification.

That summer before secondary school, we built a den among the bramble bushes with things we pinched from the allotments behind – wood, corrugated iron, even a half-height ladder. In the park, we played the same passage of football again and again – like an action replay – with me running down the wing and crossing for him to head the ball. Even now, when I'm playing five-a-side, every time I look up I expect to see that blonde head.

When the old man with the cast-eye found our den (we'd helpfully written our names on one of the boards with black marker), Jack's dad gave me a look I'd never seen from an adult before. It was as if only the thinnest layer of skin was keeping his rage inside. 'Leave,' he said, and I did. It was only years later that I realised that I was abandoning Jack.

Smaller things took on significance too. There was the plastic sheet on Jack's mattress, which I plucked at and made some joke about. You know, something about baby-proofing. And it took him a couple of seconds before he laughed.

There was also the way he'd come around to my house and watch me play computer games. He'd be fully invested in it, level after level, but he'd never take the controller. I should have questioned that. Then there was the time when he went into the fridge and lifted out a beer, even though we'd both decided that we didn't like the taste of it after that afternoon when his dad tipped his bottle at our lips and we had to splutter, had to laugh.

Like I say, only wee things. Maybe they only took on significance because of Jack's problems, many years later, with drugs. Mrs Stevens from down the road had seen him in town. All she could talk about was Jack's teeth: the state of them, the gaps in the top row when he smiled. As if his problems were only dentist-deep; could be solved with a bit of drilling and a filling or two.

The drugs are one explanation, then, and his dad is another, but my worry is that Jack was my fault, my responsibility.

At the end of the summer, we went to different secondary schools. His was Catholic and mine wasn't, but that wasn't the reason for us breaking apart. It was me. I stepped away. Not as a drifting, but as a deliberate movement. Not over weeks and months, but in a cut-all-contact way. I ghosted him, I guess, although that term wasn't around back then.

There were girls in the new school, of course, who hung around at the corner by the shop, and a new set of lads to play football with. We jumped over the park fence for games of World-Cuppy. But I didn't call in for Jack and, when he showed up, I didn't cross the ball to him in the middle but, instead, checked inside and played a short pass.

For the next couple of years, I'd see him around and we'd nod to one another. He always kept a cigarette tucked up behind his ear, against his baseball cap. The girls called out to him; asking him to come over and then, in a sudden switch, hissing him away.

Then his mum moved and he went with her. Out of sight, right through until Mrs Stevens saw him in town.

And, after that, I went online to search him out and found a profile picture of him as an eleven-year-old down by the burn. I wasn't cropped out of the photo, but that was how it felt. I sat there staring at it, knowing that I should send him a message. I should ask him how he's getting on, whether he'd like to meet up. I should apologise, maybe, and say that I'm thinking of him, rooting for him, hoping that he'll make it out the other side.

tinctumutant (noun):

an animal that changes colour

You see them in tons of social media posts, eyes on the swivel and tails flicking. You'll be scrolling through photos of food and babies and then, suddenly, there's the crested snout of one beside some pouting girl. The girl will have purple lipstick and the chameleon will be the same shade. Wealth, that is. Or it'll be pinkish and some couple will be pointing at it, fingers crossed for a baby girl. Orange for a new romance; yellow for positive news at work; blue for good health, or a record half-marathon time, or a discount on a superfood smoothie. No colour for cancer, cot death, colitis. Chameleons are good-news creatures.

That makes them expensive and that, in turn, makes them of interest to Francis. He's a young chap with a curl to his hair and suits that look like they might, at a push, have been tailored. If the market was more buoyant, he'd be an estate agent. As it is, he's an entrepreneur. He's also a grafter, but that sometimes gets translated to grifter.

Now Francis uses social media, of course he does, and he's seen these chameleons. He's never slow to hitch onto a bandwagon, so he gets himself online and he searches for "them lizard things". If asked, he'd swear that he knows he's buying monitor lizards but, if truth be told, he doesn't read beyond the pricing. Thirty of them ordered in one click and our Francis already off to post that he has the colour-changers in stock, give him a holler.

There's a juice-bar he sometimes uses. For a fee, they let him set up in a corner and, for a larger fee, they allow him to bring his lizards. He has them in a bird cage – an aviary really – and they're happy under the bright lights. None of them, of course, are anything other than green, but he explains that away by saying that they have no need to camouflage when they're in a pack. He doesn't know that the collective noun for lizards is "lounge".

The early customers are sceptical, but they're half the going rate so word soon spreads. By lunchtime, Francis is down to only five lizards, so he orders himself another thirty on rush delivery. Then he picks up the final five and takes them back to the flat. Through the evening, he sells them on social media. The buyers turn up at his door with cash. He invites one girl, with eyebrows threaded up like she's expecting a question, to join him for an amaretto cocktail. She says no.

It's still a successful day, though, and Francis begins the next by hiking up the price. With a fresh delivery of lizards, he's back at the juice-bar by lunchtime. He has a homemade sign that says "Korma Chameleon". The mistake is pointed out to him and his day only gets worse from there.

He only manages to sell one before his customers from the previous day start to show up. They want refunds. One of them slept with his boss and the bloody thing didn't turn orange; another went to the gym for the first time in two years and her chameleon didn't show the slightest bit of blue. The most damning one, though, is the couple who won big on a scratch card overnight. How are you supposed to share that news with the world if your lizard remains stubbornly green?

Francis gives six refunds in total and then beats a hasty retreat. He goes back to the flat with an aviary filled with thirty-five monitor lizards. Before he even sits down he edits his social media posts – all chameleons are now delivered direct to the customer's door and there are "no returns, no reruns". Francis knows the word refund, he's just flustered.

He makes himself a wine spritzer and drinks it through a straw. It calms him down. With the money from the day before against the delivery invoices, he's breaking even. And he's still got thirty-five lizards in his kitchen. Get them shifted and then go to ground. He has no need to ever go back to the juice-bar; they won't miss him.

There's a knock at the door. He frowns and something about the movement of his eyebrows reminds him of the customers from the night before. He goes to the peephole and, sure enough, it's the girl.

'Shit,' he hisses.

'Heard that, genius,' she calls out. 'What the fuck is this anyway? Is it a newt?'

He doesn't open the door, but the girl stays outside and she's soon joined by another customer. Francis hears him saying that he's had a promotion at work but his chameleon stayed green. That sparks an idea. He runs to the kitchen and scrabbles through the spices in the cupboard. The tiny bottles tinkle. At the back is the one he's looking for – turmeric. He's never used it, but a magazine told him it was good for muscle-repair.

When he opens the door, the girl has her lizard in his face right away, but he manages to get them inside. He takes the man's lizard first and brings it through to the sink. He sprinkles it with turmeric and, bingo, the scaly skin takes on a bit of colour. Back through it goes and the man is out the door with it, already bringing his phone out of his pocket to take the photo. That leaves the girl with a bit less wind in her sails. If you'd stayed for that drink, Francis tells her, maybe your lizard would be orange by now.

The yellow worked well, but Francis knows he needs a bit of variety. As soon as the girl takes her refund and leaves, he goes to the supermarket. Purple is *Ribena*, so that's easy enough, and he gets a couple of bags of *Wotsits* in the hope that the orange dust will do the job. From there, though, he's struggling. He sees some red food colouring –

to make pink – but all he can find for blue is acrylic paint. He stands with it in his hand for a couple of seconds, before dropping it into the basket. Pots of yellow, purple, orange and pink follow. The *Ribena* and *Wotsits* go back on the shelf.

For the rest of the afternoon, Francis deals with the line that forms at the door to his flat. Underneath his online posts are comments with his address and the juice-bar has put up a notice with it on as well. No matter, all he has to do is listen to the gist of the complaint and then shuttle the lizard back to the kitchen for the painting and hairdryer treatment. One or two refuse the colourful result, but most are happy enough as long as they have something for their photos. He even begins to sell to some new customers.

He's given out five of the blue and orange, four of the purple, and two of the pink and the yellow when it happens. He's painting a return purple when he glances across at the aviary and sees the cage lid open. There are only a handful of lizards in there, which seems odd, so he steps away from the sink and he sees them – a dozen or more – swaying their way across the lino. Their skin is flared red. He doesn't need to look at the paint pots to know that he didn't buy red. He backs up against the sink, but the purple one is there and he feels its talons pierce the skin between his neck and his shoulder. He screams and flings it to the ground. It leaves a purple splat, but manages to right itself. Then, as one, the lizards open their mouths wide and let out a hiss that sends Francis scampering for the door.

umbratic (adj.):

confined to the shade or to retirement; retired, secluded

Great Uncle Arlo has never been a pilot or worked for the airlines. He didn't fly fighter jets in the war – in any war – and when he visited relatives in Canada in the Seventies, he did so by boat.

'Please keep your seatbelts loosely fastened in case of unexpected turbulence.'

I lean over him and click the clasp of one belt into the buckle of another. Tasha came up with the idea of knotting three of them together, to stretch around his armchair like a seatbelt.

'Shows the position you must adopt when you hear *brace, brace.*'

'I'm going off to work soon, Arlo,' I say. 'But Tash is around.'

He mumbles something. It is probably a snippet of safety briefing, but I stoop closer on the off-chance that it's a moment of lucidity.

'Cabin crew, doors to automatic, cross-check and report.'

The only time I can remember being on a plane with Arlo was in the Nineties. A year or two after I'd joined his distribution business. We'd flown from Glasgow to Ireland to see Arlo's sister, my grandma, who wasn't keeping well.

After take-off, Arlo turned to me. It was late in the evening, the lights of the city were stitched out as threads of silver and gold through the black beneath us.

'We gaze up at the fucking stars,' he said, 'but how many of these eejits are looking down, out the window? Look at that fucking sight, Jamie. *We* did that. Those constellations are *ours.*'

He'd had a few whiskies while we waited for our gate

to display. Enough to see him slumped against the window, snoring deeply, by the time we landed.

Arlo used to joke that his bones had seams of coal running through them, from his time working in the mines of Fife. Even after he bought his first truck – and his second, third, fourth – the pick-axe memory of his years down the pits kept chipping at his shoulder.

When his niece, my mother, came over to Stirling University, he took to giving her weekly lectures about the working man. He didn't relent until the day, in October '72, when the Queen came to visit the campus and was booed. He'd liked that, had Arlo. The buses started driving right past my mother, standing at the entrance to the university with books under her arm and a satchel at her side. She was distraught. Arlo was delighted.

'Please make sure your seat backs and tray-tables are in an upright position.'

'There's a frost coming,' I try. 'Might need to think about changing the tyres on the trucks, especially for those driving north.'

'Your seatbelt is fastened, adjusted…'

'It's a cold spell.'

'…and unfastened as shown.'

I've asked about Arlo's fascination with the safety briefing. He had no children of his own and, with my mother and grandmother having passed, I could only ask cousins and distant relatives. I even sent an email to those in Canada. Had there been an emergency landing, a spell of turbulence, that Arlo had mentioned to them? Was there a failure in the air supply? Did masks fall from the panel above his head?

No-one had an explanation for it, though. There was no reason why, at the age of seventy-nine, he'd started to refer to the windows in his wee room at the back of our house as "over-wing exits" and become pre-occupied by the idea of someone smoking in his en-suite.

Tasha comes down the stairs, smoothing a hand across her bump. It stretches the fabric of her t-shirt, which rides high to show a seam of brown skin above the waistband of her pyjama bottoms.

'Morning,' she says.

'How did you sleep?'

'Better.'

She changed everything, Tasha. After a few months of dating, I began referring to the idea of chasing eight pints a night as "pre-Tasha". Arlo, at the bar, chuckled and said that it made her sound like a tropical storm. The comment held an uncomfortable echo of the question he'd asked when he first saw her.

'Are you still ok to work from home?' I ask Tasha. 'To look after Arlo?'

Her nose crinkles. 'Should be.'

'There's no sickness?'

'Not today.'

We've been together nine years. She came across for her graduate studies and stayed for me. Through the spell when I couldn't stay sober and the months – into years – when we couldn't conceive. Through our adoption of Great-Uncle Arlo, sixteen months ago. She's been more welcoming to him than he was to her.

'Has she ever seen snow?' Arlo asked me after he'd been introduced for the first time. Back when he was still in the office every day.

'Snow?' I said. 'Of course. She's from Minnesota. They have more snow than we have rain. Chains on the wheels of their trucks, ploughs on the front of their trains.'

'You sure?'

'Positive.'

He'd paused then. Flicking through a manifest.

'I had a friend in school,' he said. 'Way back – *way* fucking back – who was from Namibia. Maybe what you'd now call an asylum seeker, maybe not. Anyway, we were playing rugby – fantastic wee winger this lad – and it starts to fucking snow. Just a light shower. But this kid stops in the middle of the pitch and stares up. Never seen fucking snow before.'

'Tasha has, though,' I repeated. 'She's from Minnesota.'

'Thought it was shavings from the clouds or something, you know.'

'Tasha wouldn't think that, she's—'

'No fucking conception of what it was.'

Tasha moves through to the kitchen. She scratches at her thighs, at the hives beneath her pyjama bottoms. I catch at her arm and smile gently.

'We'll need to tape oven-mitts to your hands,' I say.

'I need you here to stop me itching.'

'You have Arlo.'

She looks at me, then clicks on the kettle. She allows herself one cup of coffee, in the morning. After I leave, she will sit down at the kitchen table and pick at the firm's accounts.

'Will you feed him before you go?' Tasha asks.

'Tash…'

'Please.'

I pace backwards and crane my head around the doorframe.

'Honey or jam on your toast, Arlo?'

'Cabin crew, ten minutes to landing.'

'Honey or jam?'

'Give him honey,' Tasha says.

'Why?'

93

'Better for him. Medicinal, even.'

As Tasha brews the coffee, I slide two pieces of bread into the toaster and then cut the honeyed-toast into thin strips. I will nudge them past his lips and then lift his mug of coffee to moisten his chewing. It will make me late for work.

'Did you have a look at those brochures?' Tash asks.

'The leaflets?'

'Whatever you want to call them.'

I nod. There are three affordable options. There is space in each of them. We have spoken about trial periods and the logistics of shrinking his stock of possessions once again, to make them fit an even smaller room.

'Well?' Tasha prompts.

'I'll look at them today. Properly.'

'It would be good to get it sorted.'

'Yes.'

My grandma, when she eventually went into a home, turned to the wall and studied the swirl of the *Artex*. For two years. She focused on the pattern on the wall and waited.

'I'm just not sure if—' I begin.

'It's not just the space, Jamie.'

'I know.'

'I'm not sure how he'll react.'

Tasha's laptop plays its start-up chime. I move across to where she sits, smooth her hair back from her forehead and bring my lips to her skin. Then I lift Arlo's plate and mug and turn back towards his room.

There is a soft, high-pitched whine. His legs jiggle up and down. The seatbelt strains. He has brought his head down, between his knees. With his face toward the floor, he places both hands on the back of his head, palms flat. Braced for impact.

vinaigrous (adj.):

vinegary; sour-tempered

Every spring semester, at this time, they start to queue down the corridor of the English department. Dissertation students waiting for a final supervision, first-years looking for feedback on their essay. They stand outside every door, four or five deep, quietly chatting or checking their phones. Every door, that is, except for the one at the end by the fire exit. That's Professor Fulton, and they know better than to go knocking there.

Even before I arrived at the University, I knew his reputation. He caught a second-year texting during a lecture, so he confiscated the phone and spent the rest of the hour reading out messages from the lad's mother. At Faculty meetings, he introduced something called the "fist of boredom". Simple concept, really: if he's bored, he pounds his fist against the table until they move on to the next agenda item. For conferences, he always stands at the end of panels and says, 'How are you wrong? Let me count the ways…'

All of that should make him a pariah – some of it is undoubtedly bullying and harassment – but he's tolerated because he's a titan in the field of Modernist Literature. He produces monographs faster than the rest of us can mark essays and he seems to bring in grants as readily as I stack up missed deadlines.

Which is why I need to – briefly – ignore the queue outside my office and go to knock on his door. Today is the last day for sabbatical applications, and I need his signature. In the time I spend hesitating in the hall, I know another dozen or so emails will have landed in my inbox and another two students have joined my line. One of them, Matt, catches my eye and asks if I'm alright. I try a smile and nod. I'm a Lecturer, for christ-sake, an expert in my own field, not some trembling undergrad.

Tucking my hair behind my ears, I raise my hand to the door.

'I can hear you out there,' Fulton calls. 'Shit or get off the pot.'

I lower my hand and think about whether that's an invitation to come in or not. I decide it is; it has to be if I want his signature on my application. So I turn the handle and enter.

He's in an armchair off to the side, with a standard lamp behind. There's a book propped open on his lap. From his computer comes the sound of soft jazz – Coltrane maybe – but the screen is black. He's notorious for ignoring emails or replying to them with a paper memo through the internal mail.

'Dr Jenkins,' he says, 'you decided to shit.'

I blink at him. It takes me a couple of moments to join the dots. You might expect him to smile – to show that it's a joke – but he doesn't. His shirt bulges open at the buttons to show his vest, his trousers ride high at the ankles to show his socks. Surprisingly, they have that cartoon Tasmanian Devil on them.

'Could I have your signature, please?' I hold out the application with one hand and smooth down my skirt with the other.

'Everyone always wants something,' he says, holding out his hand.

I could make a waspish response: that colleagues rarely ask anything of him; that students aren't lined up outside his door; that it's his job. Instead, I smile. He takes the application and starts to read it over.

This wasn't expected. He was only meant sign it. I think of the Senior Lecturer who moved to America a year ago.

Fulton had printed out a journal article of his and left sheets of it stacked in the cubicles in the Gents. Then he'd taken away the loo roll.

I try to think about something else, but that leaves me focusing on his ear-hair. There are great grey tufts of it. He could transplant it onto the thinning patch on top.

He looks up, I divert my eyes.

'They've asked you to add all this bollocks about engaging with local schools?'

I try not to compare his raised eyebrow to his ear-hair; darker but just as wispy.

'It'll be good for the research,' I say.

'Horse shit. All you need is the archive and some time to fucking write.'

'That's what the sabbatical is for.'

'Exactly, not this schools shite.'

'What do you want me to say?' I try to hold his gaze. 'Yes, they made me put in the outreach stuff, but it's not the worst thing to do.'

'Slippery slope,' he says, but he reaches into his shirt pocket for a pen and clicks it open to sign the application.

'Thank you,' I say, taking it. He holds on, tight enough that I think the paper might rip. Maybe he wants me to hand in a sellotaped sabbatical form. It's not the worst thing he's ever done.

'This is for the Autumn semester?' he asks.

I nod.

'Word of advice, then,' he lets go of the sheet and leans back. I think of all the "advice" he's given others in the past: telling doctoral students to go back to shelf-stacking; suggesting that the Admissions Officer purchase an abacus; interrupting a poetry reading to invite the poet to exhume the graves of Yeats and Shelley so that she might see them twisting and turning at the sound of her verse.

'Of course,' I say, holding the signed application to my chest.

'I'll be retired when you come back from sabbatical, you see…'

'Oh, that's a great sh—'

He waves this away. 'I know I'm despised, Dr Jenkins.'

'No, despised is – no.'

'Listen, though,' he peers at me. 'That's the way I want it. That's the way it needs to be. You build yourself a reputation as unapproachable, as a bit of a dinosaur, and everyone stays the fuck away.'

He reaches over to his desk and lifts a pair of spectacles. They have a glob of glue on one of the legs. I realise it's the first time I've seen them since four months ago, when he stood up in the middle of a Research Office PowerPoint presentation, took them off, snapped them, and walked out.

'We get asked to do so much,' he says. 'They treat academics like fucking vending machines. So all I'm saying is, leave their packet of crisps hanging once in a while, make them think their hand's going to get stuck.'

I don't critique his metaphor. If a student gave me it in an essay then it would have a red line through it and a question mark in the margin. All the same, there's something to what he's saying: if I didn't have a line of students outside my door then I could prepare for my afternoon seminar; if I hadn't had those research outreach meetings then my sabbatical application wouldn't have been written in the hours before bed.

'Just that word of advice,' he says and then he gives me a slow wink. It takes so long that I wonder if he's having a stroke. 'It would be a shame to see a girl as lovely as you turn as haggard and bitter as the rest.'

I feel my shoulders lift with something like relief. Just for a second, I'd thought he was right, thought he was decent.

'Professor Fulton,' I say. 'I've always found that if it walks like a dinosaur and roars like a dinosaur then it's probably a fucking dinosaur. And, if in doubt, you can tell by the stench of its breath.'

I'm shaking a little, but I still have a firm grasp of my signed sabbatical application.

He unfolds his gluey spectacles and slides them onto his nose. 'Better,' he says.

'Happy retirement,' I say, as I open the door. Then, as I close it behind me, 'You odious little wanker.'

whunk (noun):

*a dull hollow sound, as of a bullet striking something
(apparently only in the work of Hemingway)*

Hemingway used the word in *Green Hills of Africa*. He used
it twice, so it was no accident, and it was in the serialized
version as well as the final book. A simple compound word
– whistle and thunk – with an echo to the end of it.

When was the first time he thought of it? On that safari,
perhaps, or when he was an ambulance driver during the
First World War. Was the noise that of a bullet going into
the thick hide of a rhino or lodging in the frame of his
ambulance cab as he sped through the streets of Milan. That
context makes a difference, does it not?

Maybe it's this word that accounts for his tempestuous
marriages, and for that Red Cross nurse who jilted him. A
couple of glasses down and he'd start harping on, yet again,
about the precise sound of a bullet hitting the wooden lintel
over your shoulder or ripping into the calf of a running soldier.
There's no dictionary word for it, he'd say and Agnes or
Hadley or Pauline would lay a hand on his arm and say, *hush
now, Ernest, it's not something to get worked up over*.

He tried to shoehorn it in to *The Sun Also Rises*,
perhaps, but it didn't fit and his editor for *A Farewell to
Arms* quietly scored out the nine instances of it. It wasn't a
word, so it didn't make it into the novel.

That whole set in Paris had to hear about it – Ezra
Pound, Pablo Picasso, Ford Madox Ford. Each of them
nodding thoughtfully over their absinthe spoons – *that is
the noise, yes, as it hits the hunted deer or peppers the
barracks wall* – but they soon forgot. Poor Ernest couldn't
shake it, though. He heard it at night, it wrenched his
eyelids open just when they seemed to be heavy with sleep.
It was his green fairy, his shell-shock.

On fishing trips, or in the bar, he'd often return to that familiar refrain. *The precise noise*, he'd say, *the exact sound*. In Key West by then and unsettled in family life, looking at the sideboard and imagining a bullet shattering the china, watching the dog by the hearth and that soft flesh rising and falling as it snored.

The safari trip to East Africa was concocted to test his neologism. He'd listen for the noise of the bullets in the Serengeti – if it was the same for water buffalo and zebras, for giraffes and gazelles. Against the dust, against the dry grass, he'd fire his shotgun shells and listen, take notes. The fever he contracted, along with dysentery, only deepened his conviction. This was the onomatopoeic word for the moment of the bullet hitting. No ricochet.

So it went into *Green Hills of Africa* and the editor in New York let it pass. Maybe he didn't have a dictionary to hand, or perhaps he had a heavy head from the night before. It could be, even, that he realised that this wasn't Hemingway's finest work – wasn't a patch on the stories – and so the manuscript got less attention, less red ink.

On Hemingway went to the Spanish Civil War, to Cuba, and to his third marriage. Plenty of conflict, and every time he heard a bullet hit – or imagined the act of firing – he had the thought: *there's a word for that, there's my word for that*. There's a confidence to that – it engenders an arrogance – and he sought out situations in which he might hear the sound repeated, in bullet staccato. The Blitz in London and the Normandy landings in France. His fourth wife also had to be told of this word, of how apt it was – the perfect terse, taut word to give not just the noise of the striking bullet but also to intimate the moment of silence afterwards. That moment that comes before a sob of relief, a scream of agony, or the slump of death.

Then, later in life, tormented by failing eyesight and by

a conviction that the FBI were watching, Hemingway sat in the foyer of his home with a shotgun and stared down the barrel. He knew the sound as it hit other objects, other living things, but would it be the same for him? He wouldn't be able to note it, wouldn't be able to tell anyone, but at least he'd know. And the word itself would be left behind – that was his legacy – in the *Green Hills of Africa*, even if only there.

And what if the New York editor had questioned its usage, what then? Would the shotgun have been turned on that editor, maybe, in his office with the piled manuscripts, the cigar in the ashtray, and the view – if you stood at the right angle – of the Chrysler building. Would Ernest have travelled up from Florida, if the editor sent back a note which said, *no such word: try thwack or thud, clonk or crack*. Shotgun in his suitcase, would Ernest have taken to his car and driven up the Eastern seaboard?

The editor would look up from his desk, grinning at the sight of Hemingway but with a quick fade as he saw the shotgun. He'd start to speak, but Ernest would step forwards and fire a bullet into the plaster above his head. Close enough for the editor to feel the trajectory of it, to hear the whistle and ring of it along with the *whunk* as it hit the wall. Then Ernest would pause, just for a beat, before asking: *that's the very noise, wouldn't you say?* And the editor would nod, reach out to take the editorial notes from Hemingway – the notes about thwacks and thuds, clonks and cracks – and tear them to strips that would settle down by the plaster dust on the carpet.

Hemingway, satisfied with his powers of persuasion, would turn then and stride out of the office. The word would appear in *The Green Hills of Africa* and he could go listening for it in those wartime battlefields and executions, coups and massacres. It would appear for ever more in his carefully crafted prose, with no need for him to seek confirmation as to whether the editor's head accepted a bullet with the same sound as plaster or gazelles, as an ambulance cab or the calf of a running soldier, as a rhino hide or a hunted deer. That experiment could be kept for years later, in the quiet of his home, and that moment – after the noise itself – when he'd know, once and for all, if he got it right.

xenodochial (adj.):

given to receiving strangers; hospitable

When Libby saw hitchhikers on that stretch of road, by the side of Loch Lomond, she squeezed her eyes shut. *Don't stop, don't stop, don't* – and the car would slow to a stop. Her mum would dip her head out of the passenger window, or her dad would lean across. Then Libby would have to move along in the backseat and be driven thirty miles, in the wrong direction, in the company of some fragrant vagrant with a backpack that jutted, shifted and slid around like a kicking toddler.

Hitchhiker season started in March or April, with the daffodils, and ran through until the first frost. Those who only wanted a lift were bad enough, but what Libby dreaded most was the question her mum would ask after a mile or so: 'Do you have a home for the night?'

Single travellers went in the spare room, but if there were two then Libby moved to the blow-up on her bedroom floor and had to listen to a stranger squirming in her sheets; snoring, muttering, farting.

Some of them were nice, of course. There was the Dutch girl who taught Libby how to braid hair and the American who gave her fudge and a pile of creased bridal magazines. There was even that English boy with the chipped tooth. Libby had stared at it every time he smiled.

The majority were a nuisance, though. Her mum would always cook them a "hearty" dinner – mince and potatoes, kedgeree, pasta bake – and Libby would only be given the smallest portion until it was certain that the visitors had eaten their fill. It was the same at breakfast: "family hold back". The expensive muesli should be left for the Canadian, the German might like the last of the brown sugar in his tea, yes there were a half-dozen eggs but the Japanese couple might be hungry after all their sightseeing.

Libby never learnt their names, there was no point, but she would rehearse a description of them in case the police should need it. *He was taller than the bathroom door, had to stoop.* Or, *he had blond hair that was thin enough to see his scalp.* Or, *she looked innocent, yes, but she had a mole on the side of her nose and I heard her cursing at the cat.*

Her dad waved her away when she questioned the safety of it all. He would hold up the coal scuttle and smile, telling her it was all the protection they needed. But would a scuttle be any use against a knife? Or against two brothers from Morocco? Or against a gun?

At night, Libby would lie awake – in her bed or on the blow-up – and listen to the laughter from downstairs. Her mum gave them sherry, her dad offered whisky. Libby had never tried either, but she knew that whisky increased the volume and sherry made people slur their words. Both of them stopped her parents from looking at the clock, from realising it was a school-night, from raising a finger to their lips or suggesting that they should retreat into the kitchen and shut the door.

When the middle-aged man from Dumfries, with the tattoo of a cross behind his ear, left a needle on the side of the sink beside Libby's toothbrush, she thought that her dad would finally have to listen. Instead, he told her that she should never pick up a dirty needle, no matter where it was. Her mum told her that she shouldn't be so judgemental, that she'd understand when she was old enough to go travelling.

As Libby grew older – fourteen now and canny – she took to testing the new arrivals and the limits of her parents' compassion. She would wait until a hitchhiker was asleep and then pour a glass of water onto the mattress; to see if they'd admit to it. Or she'd slip her mum's antique carriage clock into a backpack and wait to see if it was discovered as missing. It always quietly made its way back to the mantel, though, and a sodden mattress was laughed off as the inevitable effect of the alcohol.

The only hitchhiker who'd ever been thrown out, as far as Libby knew, was the lad from Wales. Quite a few years before. For some reason, she didn't hold a description of him in her memory but could only have told the police about his silhouette, standing framed in her bedroom doorway. The way he breathed as if trying to clear a blocked nose. The movement of his hand, quickening. Then the sound of her dad's voice and her door being gently shut.

Libby had checked, the next morning, for blood on the edge of the coal scuttle, but there was nothing. No Welsh lad at breakfast and no mention of the night before. Everything continued as normal.

Through the winter after she turned fifteen, Libby made a decision. As soon as the snow thawed, she told her parents that she didn't want any more hitchhikers in the house: no more blow-up mattress, no more sharing cereal, no more going without a shower in the morning so that there was hot water for the guests. They listened, but they were the adults so the compromise was on their terms: she wouldn't have to share her room, they'd shut the kitchen door, they wouldn't pick up single men of a certain age.

It lasted until May. Then they brought back a man from the South of France. They left the kitchen door open as they picked at a cheeseboard and drank sherry. And then, the next week, an American girl with an adenoidal snore was sleeping on the blow-up beside Libby's bed.

Ironically, there were no backpacks in the house. So Libby took her school-bag and filled it with a couple of changes of clothes. She could only find twenty-eight pounds in cash and loose change, so she took the antique carriage clock as well. For a moment, she held the coal scuttle in her hand – considering – but she decided against it.

106

At the bottom of the driveway was the bus stop where she caught the 305 out to Loch Lomond. Then she walked across to the A82 and watched the traffic. She held her thumb out only to cars with number plates with letters that made a word – or the start of a word – because those would be easier to remember. And she told herself that, when a car stopped, she would take a second to make a judgement about whether they were coal-scuttle, abandoned-needle, doorway-silhouette or hair-braiding, bridal-magazine, chipped-tooth. She'd had plenty of practice in telling the difference.

The only car she would struggle with, the only one that would leave her with a difficult decision, was that familiar grey hatchback that travelled up and down this road every day. The one with the woman who dipped her head out of the window, the man who leant across. Libby didn't know if she was prepared to accept a lift from them.

yearsman (noun):

a labourer hired or paid by the year

Towards the end of his shift, Shaun reached into the drawer beneath the security desk and took out a stack of cards. One with a cartoon of an old man on a Zimmer, another with a dinosaur drawn by his grandson, and one with '64' on it in bubble writing. He propped that one at the front, so Mr Winterton would see it when he arrived for the day.

Shaun finished at eight in the morning, by which time he would have spent twelve hours alternating between strolling through the empty building and sitting in his swivel chair, by the monitors, with a novel. He was a voracious reader, Shaun, but quite particular in his tastes. He didn't like crime or thrillers, and certainly not fantasy. It was writers like Elizabeth Strout and Anne Tyler he loved; stories where the everyday seemed to fracture.

At twenty to eight, as normal, Winterton beeped himself into the lobby. He was Head of Fraud at the bank, up on the fourth floor. A man who constantly lost his tie-pin or misplaced his briefcase, but didn't realise because his personal assistant simply "found" them by visiting *Fortnum & Mason*. He made a point of always greeting Shaun by name. It was almost enough to make Shaun feel guilty for lying.

'Morning, Shaun.'

'Morning, sir.'

Winterton paused, mid-stride. 'Birthday today, is it?'

'Yesterday, yes.'

'Sixty-four?'

And here came the lie. 'Yes.'

'Many happy returns,' Winterton smoothed his tie, and the tie-pin slipped down. 'We'll have to think about your retirement, I suppose.'

'Plenty of time for that.'

Winterton nodded and made for the lifts. Shaun waited until they slid closed and then swept the cards from the desk. He'd been using the exact same ones for the past eight years now. It had indeed been his birthday yesterday, but he'd turned seventy-one.

The bank had a strict policy on employees retiring at sixty-five, but the job on the nightshift suited Shaun. Not only because the salary was more than the pittance of a pension, but also because he liked the reading time and the quiet thrum of the building while the city outside the glass underwent its night-time costume changes.

At the end of his shift, he went home and ate a fried breakfast. Then he slept through until the last bell at Tyler's school. His grandson was too old for drawing dinosaurs now, but Shaun treasured the couple of hours they spent together before dinner. He took him go-karting on a Monday, swimming on a Tuesday, to football on a Wednesday, the cinema on a Thursday and, usually, out for some sort of special treat on a Friday. He didn't see him at the weekends because that was Tyler's time with his dad.

All of it was for Tyler, then, and Shaun knew that if he gave up the security gig then they wouldn't be able to do even half the things they did now. Instead, he'd sit and watch the clock until school got out and then they'd sit and watch the telly until Tyler's mum collected him on the way home from her work.

Two days after his seventy-first birthday, Shaun went into work and found a card on his desk. Inside was a birthday message – "happy sixty-fourth" – and a scribble of signatures from Winterton's team. Most of them would have had to whisper-ask who the card was for and then, when told it was for Shaun, whisper-repeat *who*...? They all arrived at nine, after he'd gone home, and left at five, before he clocked in. The building was empty now, except for Grant from the dayshift, who was gathering his things to go home.

Tucked into the envelope was a thirty-pound book token. Winterton's PA would have run out to get it. She was the most likely to catch on that his sixty-fourth birthday was repeating annually, but she'd only been around for three of them. Besides, her predecessor had been fired with the memorable line, 'You're supposed to be the oil, not the bloody squeak.' Winterton didn't like to be questioned or contradicted.

Satisfied that he'd stayed his execution for another year, Shaun slid the card into his drawer and took out his phone. He sent a single text, with the words "come at ten", then folded open his copy of *Saint Maybe* until the spine cracked. As he began reading, Grant from the dayshift beeped himself out and Shaun was left to his own devices.

He paced out the fourth floor at half-nine, just to make sure, and then returned to the lobby and disabled the entry-gates. He clicked open the front door and then sat at his desk and looked at the monitors. He didn't need to do anything about the feed; it would be taken care of.

At three minutes to ten, two men pushed open the front door. Shaun recognised the one on the left, he'd been coming every year, but the one on the right was new. He was young and twitchy and had one of those undercut hairstyles where it was shaved on the sides and long on top. The man on the left gave Shaun a nod and then handed over a brown envelope.

The men stepped over to the lift. Shaun watched on the monitors, waiting for the moment that the doors slid open on the fourth floor. They used to bring equipment, a small case of tools, but now all they carried was a few USB drives. It was the younger man who busied himself on Winterton's computer. While they were there they would fix the security feed and alter Shaun's personnel file – flick his date of birth forward a year – so that he could enjoy his sixty-fourth birthday for a ninth time.

Shaun looked at his watch: five past. It would only take them ten minutes. If it was just the young guy, then something might be forgotten – the feed, the personnel file, a USB drive even – but the experienced guy was there to keep an eye. Shaun didn't need to worry. He sat back in his swivel-chair and opened the envelope to count the cash.

It was all there. He lifted his book from the desk and placed the envelope inside the front cover. He was almost finished this one, only a couple of chapters to go. He'd be done with it tonight and then, when he got home, it could go up on the shelf with the others.

zoogenic (adj.):

formed by or derived from animals or their parts

Glik was to have a pig gristle nose. That set him apart from the rest of us on Ward III, with our full thickness grafts or pedicles attached in advance of an operation. He was scheduled to actually have some foreign matter under his new skin, not just shrapnel or catgut sutures.

His nose wasn't the only point of difference, either. He spoke next to no English and only the odd word of French, so he rarely joined in with our hi-jinks. Instead, he'd sit sullenly on his bed, watching, as Freeman rode his bicycle through the ward – bell dinging – or Simpson and Jones brought their tennis game indoors to avoid the drizzle. There was little wrong with the raucous spirit of the airmen in the hospital, even if they had suffered the most horrific of injuries.

Clean the burned area with saline, then dress with penicillin cream. Apply tulle gras and gauze. Repeat twice daily and once through the night.

There was a barrel of pale ale on the ward, but Glik never partook in the drinking of it. It was watery stuff, mostly to keep us hydrated, but he only sipped at tea. On the odd occasion he might nod to a nurse when she was changing the flowers by his bed or as she lifted the wire cage to put more coke on the fire, but never more than that. Never the bawdy comments of the others; the hand stretching out of bed to pinch at a bum; the attempts to steal a kiss in the corner of the cedarwood hut once the surgical staff had left for the evening.

He was mobile enough – most of us were – and went for strolls around the grounds or, if he could hitch a lift, up in Ashdown Forest. And he was a willing listener, if we wanted to tag along and talk about the glycol igniting, or

112

struggling to wrench the cockpit canopy open, or hurtling down towards the sea with fingers so scorched they couldn't grip the parachute release. He'd listen and he'd nod and he'd pass a hand across the lump of bandages in the middle of his face.

Take the skin for the pedicle from the shoulder. A Thiersch graft. Roll from donor site into pedicle then stitch to graft site. Leave for six to eight weeks to attach.

We became a regular sight around East Grinstead. In our uniforms, yes, but with lots of new paraphernalia too: drip-stands as walking sticks, silk scarves to cover the gauze. And those pedicles, like thin elephant trunks running from our cheeks to our shoulders. Glik had one, but he turned that side of his face to the wall or held up a book to hide it. The books were in English, so we doubted he could read them.

The rest of us had no such qualms about being seen. We walked up through Blackwell Hollow, a troop of us, to the Whitehall Dining Rooms. Some of us had hands so gnarled that we couldn't light a cigarette and others needed a constant mop-up job around the eyes because their eyelids had shrunk away, but we made do. We could still dance – the majority of us – and the nurses were willing partners – again, for the most part.

When the skin flap is ready, build up the nose with pig gristle and secure in place with the graft and catgut sutures. The aim is for tension, pressure and immobilisation across the graft.

We watched Glik get his new nose. A group of us accompanied him as his bed was wheeled out across the courtyard and into the operating theatre. From the balcony, we cheered him on as Hunter put him under. He lay there on the slab and all was quiet. Then, as McIndoe wielded the knife, one of the chaps – Simpson maybe – began to *oink* and soon the whole theatre was filled with the sound of it. McIndoe called out to tell us we were "bloody fools" but he was smiling beneath his surgical mask, we could tell.

After that, Glik left the hospital for a spell. He was at a convalescent home, I suppose, or perhaps he had some family in the country. Either way, we felt his absence. The hoodlums needed their balance. There needs to be a lull in the storm, from time to time. Glik's silent presence, in the corner, had kept some of the airmen from the worst excesses: the ruining of gardener Bill's begonia bed, the damage to the leaded window at the Whitehall, the decree that Freeman and Jones should wear hospital blues as punishment for conduct unbecoming.

There was a feeling that none of that would have occurred if Glik had been present. He was a salve, a bucket of cold water. So we were delighted to hear that he was coming back for a tidy-up a few short months after the initial operation.

Lacemaker's fingers are needed, to tuck the skin in at the side and to cut away any blebs or haematomas. The goal is to provide shape and definition.

As soon as the dressing came off, Glik took to admiring his nose from a variety of angles with a hand-held mirror. He still didn't speak, but he was never done grinning. The nurses took to giving him little peck-kisses on his nose as they passed his bedside.

He no longer contented himself with watching from the sidelines either. If there was a piece of jazz on the gramophone then he was the first one up dancing and he'd always be at the table if we were dealing out a pack of cards. He still rarely took a glass of beer, but it wasn't unheard of anymore.

And, in this way, he came to be present at the founding of the Guinea Pig Club. In that cedarwood hut off to the side of Ward III. It was intended primarily as a drinking club, yes, but also as a means of supporting one another and keeping in touch as we drifted off, back to civilian life or to instructor roles in the airforce. Glik was essential to that side of things – the camaraderie – because he was steady and he was undaunted. He was also the first of us to be rebuilt not only from recycled parts of ourselves but from breakfast meat.

In those first meetings, we decided that the secretary should be a member with badly burned fingers, so that he couldn't take minutes, and that the treasurer should have hash-browned legs, so that he couldn't abscond with the funds. There was quite a bit of laughter about all that and, when it settled down, someone looked across at Glik – good old Glik – and asked him what role he would like to take on in our new club.

'I am...' he said, haltingly. Then he tapped the side of his pig gristle nose. '... the sommelier.'

About the Author

Liam Bell is author of three novels, with the most recent being *Man at Sea*. His debut novel was shortlisted for the SMIT Scottish Book of the Year and he has featured as Paperback of the Week in the *Herald* and at the 2014 Edinburgh International Book Festival. Short stories and articles have appeared in publications including *New Writing Scotland*, *Litro* and *Northwords Now*. He was born in Orkney, grew up in Glasgow, and is now Senior Lecturer at the University of Stirling, where he is Programme Director of the MLitt in Creative Writing. He lives in Scotland with his wife and two young daughters. More information at www.liammurraybell.com or on twitter @liammurraybell.

Like to Read More Work Like This?

Then sign up to our mailing list and download our free collection of short stories, *Magnetism*. Sign up now to receive this free e-book and also to find out about all of our new publications and offers.

Sign up here:
   http://eepurl.com/gbpdVz

Please Leave a Review

Reviews are so important to writers. Please take the time to review this book. A couple of lines is fine.

Reviews help the book to become more visible to buyers. Retailers will promote books with multiple reviews.

This in turn helps us to sell more books… And then we can afford to publish more books like this one.

Leaving a review is very easy.

Go to http://bit.ly/3yZrQDw, scroll down the left-hand side of the Amazon page and click on the "Write a customer review" button.

Other Writing by Liam Bell

So It Is

Published by Myriad Editions

Aoife, a young girl growing up in 1980s Belfast, finds herself the last line of defence between the violence and her family. While her mother sinks deeper into a medicated stupor, and her father leaves the family for the comforts of the local bars, Aoife cares for her brother Damien, trying to keep him out of harm s way, while all around her friends and neighbours are swept up in the conflict.

Meanwhile Cassie, a Republican paramilitary and honeytrap, lures and seduces her victims, inflicting lasting damage. But her infamous tactics have their repercussions, and before long her past catches up with her.

So It Is is an unflinching and suspenseful debut that reflects the factions and fractures of the Troubles from a new perspective, culminating in a breathless sequence in which the choice between violence and personal morality becomes shockingly acute.

"Unputdownable! This is a real page turner. I found it unsettling and challenging." (*Amazon*)

Order from Amazon:

Paperback: ISBN 978-1-908434-14-2
eBook: ASIN B0081RLJ68

The Busker

Published by Myriad Editions

Three cities, two years, one chance: from the author of the critically acclaimed debut *So It Is* – shortlisted for best first book at the Scottish Book Awards 2013 – comes the hard-hitting story of a young man determined to find his voice. Plucked from obscurity in Glasgow, Rab Dillon is about to become the next great protest singer. Seduced by promises of stardom, carrying only the guitar given to him by the girl who broke his heart, he travels down to London. There he records the debut album that will speak to the dispossessed, the disenfranchised and disheartened. One year later, he is sleeping rough on the streets of Brighton.

A modern-day ballad set across three cities and two years, *The Busker* is a richly comic exposé of the music industry, the Occupy movement, homelessness, squatting – and failing to live up to the name you (almost) share with your hero. It is also the story of what survives when the flimsy dreams of fame fall apart.

Order from Amazon:

Paperback: ASIN B00RWOH0LO

Other Publications by Bridge House

The Day Chuck Berry Died
by Ian Inglis

A collection of eclectic and original short stories that bring into focus those decisive moments in a person's life whose significance may not be recognised at the time, but which often have profound and lasting impacts long into the future.

The distorted contours of human nature, as practised in the daily activities of professional footballers; the repercussions of a young man's visit to the battlefields of Flanders to visit his grandfather's grave; a surprising encounter in a Parisian cafe. Choices made on the basis of what we know – or what we think we know – which come back to torment us, challenge us, enlighten us; attitudes and behaviour we can barely comprehend; routine events and situations that bring with them periods of great sadness or unexpected happiness; confusion and clarity when long-hidden truths are finally revealed.

Order from Amazon:

Paperback: ISBN 978-1-914199-32-5
eBook: ISBN 978-1-914199-33-2

A Feast of Tales (Gently Twisted)
by Dawn Bush

A tempting tale for every mood.

An eclectic mixture of tales that take you to a pragmatic Fairyland, where anything can happen – and not all of it beneficial; to an unknown dusty planet in the distant sky; back in time on earth through time, space, land and sea; through love, selfishness and triumph. They are a feast of the unexpected.

A Feast of Tales (Gently Twisted) is an intriguing collection of short stories by Dawn Bush.

"A charming selection of stories. With some fairy tales and other contemporary stories, there is a mixture of wit and realism. But all beautifully written. Thoroughly recommended." (*Amazon*)

Order from Amazon:

Paperback: ISBN 978-1-914199-12-7
eBook: ISBN 978-1-914199-13-4

I Knew it in the Bath
by Linda Flynn

I Knew it in the Bath is a collection of absorbing short stories which show that no matter how we expect events to unfold, life has a way of confounding us. What will a woman do to save her friend? Do we really know when we're being watched? Why did Dora throw the iron through the window? What's the best way to take revenge on a cheating partner?

Settle back for an engaging read through these humorous, sinister and thought-provoking stories, but try not to drop your book in the bath!

Linda Flynn, a frequent contributor to our annual themed anthologies, gives us food for thought in the stories collected in *I Knew in in the Bath.*

"I can't recommend this anthology enough. Linda Flynn has such a way with words." (*Amazon*)

Order from Amazon:

Paperback: ISBN 978-1-914199-28-8
eBook: ISBN 978-1-914199-29-5

Ingram Content Group UK Ltd.
Milton Keynes UK
UKHW021435070423
419618UK00011B/145